THE COTTAGE IN LADY FERN LANE

DAPHNE NEVILLE

ISBN: 9798884511231

PublishNation
www.publishnation.co.uk

Other Titles by This Author

TRENGILLION CORNISH MYSTERY SERIES

The Ringing Bells Inn

Polquillick

Sea, Sun, Cads and Scallywags

Grave Allegations

The Old Vicarage

A Celestial Affair

Trengillion's Jubilee Jamboree

PENTRILLICK CORNISH MYSTERY SERIES

The Chocolate Box Holiday

A Pasty in a Pear Tree

The Suitcase in the Attic

Tea and Broken Biscuits

The Old Bakehouse

Death by Hanging Basket

Murder in Hawthorn Road

Great Aunt Esme's Pasty Shop

The Frolicsome Crystal Ball

TRENWALLOE SANDS CORNISH MYSTERY SERIES

Albert's Old House

The Old Coaching Inn

The Old Tile House

Chapter One

Standing in the front garden of Lavender Cottage amongst a spectacular display of colourful dahlias, retired gym mistress Dilly Granger snipped off the heads of faded flowers and dropped them into a bucket. As she finished the chore and placed her scissors on top of the discoloured blooms, her next door neighbour, Amelia Trewella, returned from the post office where she had been to purchase a birthday card for her husband, Ernie. With an air of excitement Amelia leaned over the green railings that separated Dilly's garden from the pavement.

"I've just seen Dotty and she told me that while out jogging along Lady Fern Lane this morning she saw a removal van pull up outside Holly Cottage, so it looks as though the new people are moving in today."

"At last! Wonderful!" exclaimed Dilly. "Once they're settled in we must pop round and welcome them to Trenwalloe Sands. Although I suppose we can't just turn up so we'll need to think of a good reason to call."

"Oh, I'm sure we'll come up with something."

"Yes, we must." Dilly considered the matter briefly, "I know what we'll do. On the off chance the new people might be in their front garden, we'll take the dogs up there for a walk. I'm sure they'll appreciate it, the dogs, that is, and if the weather's fine we can lurk around by picking blackberries. Providing there are brambles along the lane of course."

"What a good idea and yes there are but the majority might not be ripe yet. I know about the brambles, you see, because I've picked basket loads along there with Ernie in the past."

"For his blackberry wine?"

Amelia nodded. "Yes, for his blackberry wine. Oh this is so exciting. I've not been in either of the houses in Lady Fern Lane but have always admired them from outside. Especially Denzil's. His new front porch is a beauty." Amelia turned her head as a van passed by and tooted; both ladies waved on seeing the driver was the aforementioned local builder, Denzil Williams, "Well, talk of the devil," she chuckled.

"And he's bound to appear," finished Dilly.

"So true." Amelia frowned, "I do hope the new people are nice. I mean, I know Denzil's house is some distance away from Holly Cottage but all the same I bet he'll be concerned about having new neighbours."

"Were you and Ernie worried about who moved into Lavender Cottage then? Before I turned up, that is."

"My goodness me, yes. As it is the gods were looking down on us and we're blessed to have you as a neighbour."

"Flattery will get you everywhere," chuckled Dilly. "Fancy a cup of tea?"

"I'd love a cuppa. We had kippers for lunch and they were rather salty."

Dilly picked up the bucket of faded flower heads. "Good, and then you can remind me again who used to live at Holly Cottage because I've forgotten."

"Hmm, well I can't tell you a great deal and I can't even remember her name but then that's probably because we never met. She didn't socialise much, you see, because she wasn't in the best of health. Which is why she's gone into care, I suppose." Amelia stepped down from the pavement onto the pathway between the two front gardens and joined Dilly as she opened her front door.

Larry Greenwood heaved a sigh of relief as the removal van drove away down the narrow Cornish lane. Waving as it disappeared around a bend, he stepped back inside the old stone cottage and wiped his feet on the doormat. "Thank goodness we've got everything in before the rain starts. That sky looks as black as your hat." He closed the door and turned to his wife who was placing a bag marked cushions beside the couch, "Fancy a cuppa, Kate?"

"Yes, but I'll make it while you get the fire lit."

"A fire! Why? I mean, it's July."

"I know but after all the rushing around we've done today we might feel chilly later and a fire will make it feel cosier, especially if it rains. The place seems a bit damp too, but that's hardly surprising with it having been unoccupied for a year or so." She stepped towards the door leading into the kitchen. "And before you say there's nothing to burn, I remember seeing a pile of logs in the shed when the estate agent showed us around."

In their early sixties, Larry and Kate had decided to give up city life and move to the country while they were still young enough to enjoy it. Larry, who had spent his working life as a self-employed electrician, hoped to continue working part-time until he reached retirement age and was eligible for his state pension. Kate, also retired, had been a dental nurse and looked forward to having more free time. She joked that for the rest of her life she'd be happy to look in no other mouth than her own.

After looking at various locations on-line, and then viewing several houses in Cornwall, they chose Holly Cottage in Trenwalloe Sands, in Larry's case because it needed up-dating. In Kate's case it was because of the garden: in particular she loved the roses growing over a crooked arch near to the front door and the gentle stream flowing amongst the trees around the back. In the city they had had no garden: just a good sized courtyard to the rear of their semi-detached house and a narrow border to the front.

Holly Cottage had been put up for sale because the previous owner, an elderly widowed lady of eighty-four, had gone into a care home following a fall. Being pragmatic she knew it unlikely she'd ever return to her home of sixty years and so had asked her family to sell it on her behalf; the proceeds would cover the cost of her care and allow her a few of life's luxuries.

On Saturday morning, Kate was woken by sunlight streaming in through the grimy bedroom window. Surprised she had slept soundly for the first night in a new environment, she was eager to get up and continue with the unpacking. Not wanting to disturb her husband, she crept from the room, had a quick wash in the bathroom and then made her way down to the kitchen. As the kettle boiled she heard a creak from the bare floorboards on the landing. Knowing Larry liked a cup of tea before his ablutions, she popped a teabag into his favourite mug.

As he entered the kitchen she pointed to the window overlooking the back garden. "I'm taking my tea out there so I can sit in the sun on that old bench. Will you join me?"

"Happily." He picked up his mug of tea, "but before we sit on it, let me give it the once-over first. It looks pretty decrepit and I don't want it collapsing under our weight."

The stability of the bench, shabby but sound, met with Larry's approval so both sat to take in their surroundings of weeds, a few trees, several sparsely growing shrubs, an abundance of Japanese Anemones and an area of long grass which they assumed had once been a lawn.

"Bliss," muttered Kate, thrilled by the birdsong. "I think today along with the day I married you and we had our children must be one of the happiest of my life."

"I have to agree and look at that view. I could sit here and gaze over those hills and the woodland for hours."

"And so you shall once we're straight but for now there is much to be done inside and out." Kate stood. "In fact I'm not really sure where to start but I suppose the kitchen would make the most sense."

Larry tipped the dregs from his mug onto the weeds. "I agree and while you do that I'll unpack our laptops and arrange for an internet connection."

While Larry was busy in one of the two sitting rooms, Kate put away the most frequently used kitchen utensils in the solitary, free-standing cupboard by the sink. When finished she looked around with satisfaction. "This room is going to be one of my favourites," she said to her husband who, having completed his chores, carried in a box labelled cookery books. "Fantastic view, it's not too big, not too small and I love the fact we have a utility room for the washing machine and freezer."

"Yes, very handy but I notice the plaster on the outer wall is very loose so we must get that fixed before we put too much stuff out there."

Kate waved her hand around. "These walls are fine though, aren't they? So we can get on in here."

"Yes, I've had a good tap around and they seem in surprisingly good condition."

"Good. So we just need to get the flooring sorted, paint the walls and then it'll be ready for new units."

"You still want to replace the lino then?" Larry teased, "I mean, I think it's very much in keeping with the place."

"Ha ha. I take it you're speaking tongue in cheek. At least I hope you are."

"Yes, of course. It's long since seen better days and the cracks and small holes could be downright dangerous. I don't like lino anyway, not unless it's springy, and it stands to reason we need to get nice solid tiles down before we get a new kitchen fitted." He looked around the spacious square room. "Goodness knows how the previous owner managed with only the cupboard under the stairs, the utility room and the cupboard under the sink for storage. Having said that, she lived alone once widowed and probably didn't have a great deal of clutter anyway. That's the trouble today, we all have so many gadgets for the kitchen, half of which are seldom used and end up in the backs of cupboards."

To avoid commenting on the unnecessary kitchen gadgets that she was guilty of purchasing; still to be unpacked and stacked in the utility room, Kate made coffee and then sat down at the kitchen table. "I wonder what this room looked like when it was first built. In fact not just the kitchen but the whole house."

Larry took a seat opposite his wife. "Well I'm pretty sure there would have been a Cornish Range or whatever for cooking in the inglenook fireplace over there. I doubt much else has changed though other than converting the smallest bedroom into a bathroom and judging by the old fashioned suite I should imagine that was done a fair few years ago."

"Yes, you don't see many high level water cisterns these days."

"I agree although I quite like it. It reminds me of my childhood."

Kate nodded over towards the fireplace. "I wonder why it was taken out. The Cornish Range or whatever. It would have looked rather nice."

"No idea, perhaps it ceased functioning. I like the idea too so perhaps in the fullness of time we could get hold of one or something similar to fill the empty space."

"Be nice but there's no rush and I do like my electric cooker." Kate put down her coffee mug on the wooden draining board and looked out of the window. "Do you think there would have been a well out there backalong?"

"Definitely. These places were built long before houses had running water and plumbing."

"Yes, of course and I don't think they'd have used water from the stream." Kate pushed her chair back under the table. "It's so exciting and I love the fact lots of people will have lived here before us and they'll all have left their mark one way or another."

Larry drained the last of his coffee. "And as time goes on we'll no doubt find out who some of them were."

"Well, I've already done a bit of detective work and concluded that the previous owner who is now in a care home, was religious. I refer of course to where the paint is discoloured in the shape of a cross above the inglenook fireplace."

Larry turned his head to view the wall in question. "Oh yes, I hadn't noticed. Still, a good coat of paint should cover that."

Kate sighed deeply. "I'm so glad we moved here. The house feels as though it's steeped in history, much of which we'll never know."

"No, not unless you can get the walls to talk."

"Now that would be interesting."

Inside Yew Tree Cottage, Amelia Trewella stood back to admire the table she had laid for dinner. She and Ernie usually ate in the kitchen but because it was Ernie's birthday and they were to be joined by their next door neighbour Dilly, and her friend-cum-companion, Orville, she had opted to make use of their little used front room.

At half past seven, the Trewellas greeted their guests like long lost friends even though Amelia and Dilly had met for coffee at Lavender Cottage earlier in the day.

Orville's nose twitched as he stepped over the threshold. "Hmm, something smells good."

"I've played safe and made a chicken and bacon lasagne for two reasons," said Amelia, "one, I've made it umpteen times before and it's never let me down and two, because it's Ernie's favourite."

"Sounds smashing," Orville handed Ernie two bottles of merlot, "I know you make your own but these are a birthday present."

"Thank you and very welcome they are too." Ernie led the way into the front room and placed the bottles of wine on the drinks cabinet. He then poured drinks for the two guests who sat down side by side on a small, cream leather sofa.

"Cheers," Ernie raised his glass.

"Cheers" echoed Orville, "and if I haven't said it yet, many happy returns of the day."

In his late seventies, Orville King was best known for his role as leader to the Trenwalloe Sands Male Voice Choir. He lived alone in a two bedroomed bungalow on the Buttercup Field Estate, his home of two years. Prior to that he had lived in the King's family home along with his widowed sister, but on her death he felt the house was too big for one and sold it to enable him to downsize. Dilly and Orville had known each other for less than a year but during that time their friendship had blossomed. Having never married, Dilly, in the autumn of her years, was reluctant to change her marital status; a fact about which she was adamant. Nevertheless, Orville was forever optimistic that one day she would be persuaded to change her mind and always referred to her as his intended.

"Have you seen or heard anything about the new folks in Lady Fern Lane?" Ernie asked Orville.

"I've not seen them but I know Denzil has spoken to them on the phone. Apparently he's been asked to give them a quote for laying floor tiles in the kitchen so it looks like they'll be doing the old place up."

"They're not wasting any time either then," said Ernie, "they only moved in yesterday."

“So how many are there in the family or whatever?” Dilly asked.

Orville shrugged his shoulders. “Denzil didn’t say but I got the impression they were retired so it might just be two of them.”

“Well however many of them there are I hope they don’t come across any problems,” said Ernie. “That’s the last thing you want if you’re retired.”

“Problems?” Amelia was confused.

“Yes, all sorts of things come to light when old places get renovated. Doors that have been bricked up, weak joists, rot under floor boards. Dry rot even. Not to mention damp.”

“Oh yes, but there might be some nice things too,” said Dilly, cheerfully, “like jewels hidden under floorboards or long forgotten treasures. Antiques in the attic even and perhaps a nice old diary.”

“Orville rolled his eyes. “Well if I had to put any money on it, I’d have to say that Ernie’s more likely to be right.”

Chapter Two

On Monday morning, general builder Denzil Williams, whose name Larry had been given when enquiring at the post office about tradesmen in or near to the village, arrived to size up the job of tiling the kitchen floor. Larry and Kate took an instant liking to him and were further delighted to discover that he was their neighbour and lived in the only other house along Lady Fern Lane.

"So have you lived next door long?" Kate asked as they stepped into the kitchen.

"A couple of years, that's all. I bought it after the old boy who lived there died. He was a bit of a recluse and I don't recall ever seeing him. Anyway, he left the place to a nephew who was keen to get shot of it quickly and because it needed modernising, I got it for a good price. I've done a fair bit to it but there's still plenty more to do."

"So is it anything like this place?" Larry asked, "The layout, I mean."

"Almost identical, I believe. I know they were built at the same time and no doubt to the same plan and by the same builders. Needless to say both have undergone a few changes over the years though."

"We'd love to see your place, wouldn't we, Kate? If that's alright with you of course, Denzil. We're planning to make alterations here too, you see, so it'd be interesting to see what you've done so far."

Kate agreed. "We're not planning anything too drastic. Just a conservatory or patio on the back and do up the bathroom too. The old suite is looking very careworn now and we'd like a shower installed."

"We're also toying with the idea of knocking the two living rooms into one," added Larry, "but we're undecided at present."

"Ah well, I can recommend you doing that. I've done the same with my place and having light come in both back and front has made the room so much brighter. I knocked out the back window too and installed French doors."

Larry's face lit up. "Oh, I like the idea of that. Perhaps after you've weighed up the kitchen floor job, you'll give us a quote for knocking down the wall as well."

"Will do, and you're welcome to pop round to my place any time after five and I'll show you around. Today even if you like."

While Denzil measured up the kitchen floor and considered the wall removal job, Kate and Larry selected tiles from samples, then while they sat drinking coffee, Denzil did the sums and gave them a rough estimate for both jobs. It met with approval and he said he'd be able to start the kitchen floor as soon as Wednesday due to the postponement at another property of a dividing wall to create an ensuite shower room, the owner having been taken ill.

"Oh dear. I'm sorry to hear that. Hope it's nothing too serious," said Kate.

"I believe it's just a nasty chest infection. The poor bloke's in hospital but should be out by the end of the week. We'll still not be able to start the work though as he'll need to rest."

As Kate removed the coffee mugs and placed them on the draining board, Larry pointed towards the utility room. "While you're working here would you be willing to plaster the wall in there as well? It's blown in a couple of places so we don't want to clutter the room up 'til it's done."

Denzil walked into the utility room to take a look. "Hmm, lovely big space this. It would have been the washhouse with a built in copper up the corner once upon a time. It's the same as my place, you see, but the copper's obviously been taken out here to make more room so it seems much bigger than mine. I assume the chimney's gone as well."

"A built in copper with a chimney. I'd like to have seen that," said Kate.

Denzil chuckled. "Well when you come round to see my place I'll show you mine. I'm reluctant to remove it because although it's defunct, it's a piece of history." He then tapped over and around the loose plaster. "This is no problem at all. I don't specialise in plastering myself but I know a chap who does. Freddie Hewitt. I put a lot of work his way and he's very good."

"Ideal," said Larry, "and if ever you're in need of a qualified electrician I'd be happy to help out."

"Now that's music to my ears. The chap I usually use fell off a ladder last week and will be off work for several months. I was wondering what to do as I've an extension to build on Dilly Granger's place when the plans are finalised so it'll be all hands to the deck then."

"Well, I'm up for that. Does this Dilly Granger live in the village?"

"Yes, at Lavender Cottage and funnily enough she's the godmother of Freddie Hewitt the plasterer who I just mentioned. You'll like them, they're really nice people but then again so is everyone who lives here in Trenwalloe Sands."

"Everyone?" gasped Kate.

"Well, more or less."

That same afternoon, Dilly and Amelia strolled along Lady Fern Lane with Oscar and Ben on leads. Oscar, a golden retriever was a member of the Trewella family, namely, Amelia and Ernie. Ben, an aged black Labrador, became Dilly's companion late in his life following the death of his master, retired fisherman and local historian, John Martin. With John having no living relatives other than an older brother, Dilly had offered to give Ben a home; for Bruce, the older brother in question, lived in sheltered accommodation and felt he wouldn't be able to give Ben the walks and attention he would need.

As the foursome neared Holly Cottage they slowed their pace hopeful of seeing the village's newest inhabitants. But it was not their lucky day. Not only was there no car parked alongside the house but the door and windows were closed and there was no sign of life.

"Damn," groaned Dilly, "looks like they might be out."

"Oh well, all is not lost. A handful of blackberries are ripe so there's just about enough to make a blackberry and apple pie."

On Tuesday, Larry and Kate moved everything that stood on the kitchen floor to other parts of the house. The fridge they wheeled into a corner in the least cluttered sitting room along with the kitchen table and chairs. Larry disconnected the electric cooker and took it into the utility room. They placed the microwave, kettle, mugs, plates and cutlery on top of the kitchen table or underneath in boxes. Everything else they stored wherever there was a space.

The previous evening they had walked along the lane to Willow Cottage to take up Denzil on his invitation to view his opened up living space with French doors leading out into his back garden. As Denzil had claimed the large room was bright and airy and the early evening sun shone through the large window overlooking the front garden. Impressed, Kate and Larry, both in accord, expressed their keenness to have the same done to Holly Cottage but all agreed the kitchen must take priority and the removal of the dividing wall could wait until the kitchen was fully functional.

On Wednesday morning, Denzil arrived bright and early to tile the floor along with Brett, his seventeen year old apprentice. While Brett unloaded boxes of tiles and bags of adhesive from the van, Larry, eager to make himself useful, helped Denzil tear up the old lino and take it out into the back garden. Kate, however, decided to keep out of the way and went upstairs to paint the ceiling on the landing. By the end of the working day half of the kitchen floor had been transformed and the room seemed much brighter.

After Denzil and Brett left, saying they'd be back at eight the next morning, Kate made mugs of tea which she and Larry drank in the front sitting room. They then returned to the kitchen once again to admire the new part-laid floor and congratulate themselves on their choice of large, marble effect, high-gloss tiles.

"Denzil was telling me that he loves tiling floors," said Larry. "It was one of the first jobs he learned to do and he never tires of doing it. I can see his point though because in a relatively short space of time the transformation is huge."

"Well, I can't disagree with that." Kate nodded towards the cupboard under the stairs with its access from the kitchen. "It's just a thought, but while we're having the floor done in here we might as well have the tiles go out into the cupboard as well. I mean, at the moment it has the same grotty lino that was in here. I know it's had less wear and so is in better nick but it's still pretty awful. Ancient too I should imagine so it'll probably crack up before long."

Larry opened the door to the understairs cupboard. "That's a good point. We'll put that to Denzil in the morning and to save time we'll rip up the old lino ourselves."

Kate was delighted Larry readily agreed with her suggestion. "And no time like the present so we'll do it now."

When the lino was up and outside with the rest, Larry began to brush the concrete floor. As he cleared a section, a puzzled look crossed his face. “Come and take a look at this, Kate. Part of the concrete in here is a different colour to the rest. I wonder why.”

He quickly brushed away the remaining dust and shards of old lino to reveal an area clearly lighter in colour and approximately two foot square.

Kate scratched her head. “Well I’ve no idea why that might be.”

“Same here but on the other hand, do you think it might be where a trapdoor to a cellar once was?”

“No, surely not. I mean if that’s the case, why fill it in?”

“Don’t know. Perhaps it used to flood, was very damp or maybe it’s probably just wishful thinking on my part.” Larry tapped all over the lighter square with the broom handle. “I’m not sure what to say. It seems solid enough and if we chip away and there’s nothing there, it’ll delay Denzil laying tiles in here. On the other hand, if that’s the case, I suppose we could not bother him with it and do something in here ourselves at a later date.”

“Or better still we could leave it for now and see what Denzil thinks in the morning. After all he’s a general builder so might come up with a logical reason for the different shades.”

Larry agreed. “Good thinking. We’ll sleep on it and go along with whatever Denzil suggests.”

When Denzil and Brett arrived the next morning and were shown the lighter square in the understairs cupboard, Denzil agreed it could well have been the entrance to a cellar because his house further along the lane had one in the same location and it was still accessible.

“Really! What sort of size is it?” Larry asked.

Denzil cast his eyes around the kitchen. "About half the size of this room, I'd say. I must admit I've only been down mine a couple of times and so don't have anything stored there but I will do eventually after I've tanked the walls."

Larry scratched his head. "Hmm, sounds interesting, I must admit."

"So, what shall we do?" Denzil asked, "After all it's your place so the ball's in your court."

"I'm not sure," said Kate, "I'd like to know if there's anything there but at the same time I don't want to hold you up and it must have been sealed up for a reason. What do you think, Larry?"

Larry shook his head. "Not sure, but then if we don't find out now we'll forever be wondering and once the tiles are down in the cupboard it'll be too late to look into it then."

"True. How about we chip away a bit and see what's underneath the bit of lighter concrete," said Kate, "I mean, if there is a cellar it's hardly likely to have been filled in beyond the entrance."

"I'll get some tools," Brett dashed out to the van and because he was clearly itching to begin the excavation, and he was younger, they permitted him to begin the chipping. After ten minutes and several chunks of concrete later, a small area of red was visible. After thirty minutes more when all the concrete was removed, the area revealed a square of red bricks crudely surrounded by lumps of wood which looked likely to have been part of the original door frame.

Denzil stooped down to get a closer look. "Looks promising and I bet if we remove these bricks and the bits of wood we'll find steps."

With excited haste, Brett chipped away at the wood and then removed the bricks one by one. It was an easy task for they were not cemented in but merely stacked tightly together. As Denzil anticipated, under the bricks three granite steps were visible. Brett removed the goggles protecting his eyes and using the torch on his mobile phone shone the light down into the hole. Five more steps were visible below the first three.

"Very interesting," enthused Larry, "So who's going down there to explore?"

Kate shuddered. "Definitely not me. It smells musty and will be all cobwebby, damp and dark. Possibly dangerous too."

"No, it'll be safe," said Denzil, "Be different if the steps were wooden but granite should be sound enough." He turned to Brett: "Shine the torch across the ceiling, I'm wondering if there's a light in there, you see. There is in mine."

Brett did as he was asked and in the beam of light a pendula bulb was picked up dangling from the cellar's ceiling.

"Ideal," said Larry. "So there should be a light switch somewhere." He stood up and found a switch part-hidden between two shelves. He flicked it on but nothing happened.

"I suppose the bulb's no good," Kate stood up to ease her back.

"I'll go down anyway. I've plenty of power left in my battery so I'll be fine in the torchlight." Brett eagerly placed his foot on the first step.

"And I'll follow," Larry reached for his phone on the window sill and switched on its torch.

A look of concern crossed Denzil's face. "I don't think I'll join you because if it's like mine I'll know what to expect, but take it easy both of you and look where you're putting your feet because there could be bits of loose concrete, wood and brick chippings on the steps, not to mention all sorts of junk once you're down there."

"Will do," said Larry, who as an electrician was used to being cautious.

Denzil and Kate, happy to watch from a distance, knelt in the cramped cupboard space by the cellar's entrance and watched as Larry and Brett descended the steps, keeping close to the wall on the left-hand side, both eager to see what, if anything, materialised in the flickering torchlight.

"It's not too pokey down here," called up Larry, as he reached the bottom. "It feels awfully damp but at least there's room to swing a cat and it appears to go out under the hallway and the living room."

"Is there anything down there?" Kate knew it was daft but she was thinking of valuables.

"No," said Larry, "nothing of great interest anyway. There's what looks like a broken handrail which would have been on the right-hand side of the steps. It's made of wood so I should imagine it toppled over years ago. There's the remains of the old trapdoor too and quite a few rusty tools that have long since seen better days but I might be able to clean them up. Oh, and there's a tatty bit of old matting bundled in the corner."

Brett approached the matting, leaned forwards to touch it and laughed. "It's a rug but I don't think this will take pride of place on your new kitchen floor." With both hands he pulled it from the corner and shook it. The rug disintegrated into tiny fragments and from it a variety of bones, a skull, a pocket watch and an ornate wooden crucifix, tumbled onto the filthy floor.

Chapter Three

"Ah," said Larry, when he found his voice, "that probably explains why the cellar was sealed up then."

"Are they real?" Even in the dim light it was obvious Brett's face was very pale and he appeared to be shaking. "The bones, I mean. Are they real? Are they human?"

Denzil having hastily joined Larry and Brett stooped down to get a better look. "That skull is definitely human and the rest look real enough to me."

"Shall I ring the police?" called Kate from her kneeling position on the floor of the understairs cupboard, phone already in her hand and switched on.

"Yes, but don't dial 999." Larry looked at the scattered remains. "This poor sod's been dead for a while so it's hardly an emergency."

Denzil scrambled to his feet. "I'll do it, Kate, and I'll ring the local nick. I have its number because a bloke I know is a copper there although he's away on holiday at the moment."

As Denzil left the cellar, closely followed by Brett, Larry not wanting to leave fingerprints, took a tissue from his sleeve and picked up the pocket watch hoping there might be an inscription on the back to help identify the remains. To his dismay there was nothing, so with care he placed it back amongst the bones and joined everyone else in the kitchen.

With the call to the police made they sat with mugs of coffee around the table amongst the clutter in the front sitting room to await the arrival of the police, having been told to touch nothing. Within five minutes there was a knock on the front door.

"They can't be here already," Larry looked at the carriage clock on the mantelpiece.

Denzil stood up. "No, I should imagine it's Freddie come to weigh up the plastering job. With all the excitement I forgot to tell you that he said he'd call round sometime today." Denzil answered the door, invited Freddie in, introduced him to Larry and Kate and then told him what they had found.

The police arrived ten minutes later and were shortly followed by scenes of crime officers. Larry, Kate, Denzil and Brett were questioned while the forensics team examined the cellar. Freddie listened to every word in order to relay the news to his godmother, Dilly, who he knew was eager to receive any information regarding the newcomers.

After questions had been answered, the five sat around the table drinking more coffee and speaking in hushed voices as they tried to make sense of the situation. However, having very little detail to go on they were unable to come up with any suggestions as to the identity of the unfortunate owner of the bones. Larry and Kate knew the lady from whom they had purchased Holly Cottage was a widow and Denzil confirmed that she and her late husband had lived in the house for a very long time. He was also confident that the bones could not belong to the deceased husband simply because he remembered the funeral.

Eventually the police and forensic team finished their duties but before they left, they asked that work on the kitchen floor be halted for the time being in case they needed to look inside the cellar again.

On leaving Holly Cottage, Freddie drove into the village and parked alongside Lavender Cottage, the home of his godmother. He let himself in and called out as he closed the front door. "Only me, Dilly."

"Freddie." She gave him a hug. "Lovely to see you. Sit down and I'll make you a tea, or would you prefer coffee?"

"Tea will be fine, even though I've just had a coffee at Holly Cottage."

Dilly stopped, the kettle in mid-air. "You've been to Holly Cottage. Why were you there? What are the new people like? How many are there in the family and did you like them?"

"To sum up, a job, nice, two and yes."

"Sorry, I should know better than to fire away so many questions at once."

As Dilly poured water onto a teabag for her godson, the back door opened. "Co-ee, it's only me." Amelia entered the room her face flushed. "Oh, hello, Freddie. I didn't know you were here." She sat down on one of the armchairs by the Truburn and fanned her flushed face. "You're probably wondering why I'm a bit puffed and I can tell you it's because Ernie's just got back from taking Oscar for a walk and he said he saw a police car at the Back Lane junction and it went whizzing off down Lady Fern Lane. Then a few minutes later he saw a SOCO van heading in the same direction. So what an earth do you think is going on down there?"

"Really! Well Freddie might know a thing or two because he's just this minute come from there."

"You have! So what's going on, Freddie?" Amelia was on the edge of her seat.

Freddie took the mug of tea from Dilly. He then relayed the events as he knew them.

On Saturday afternoon, while strimming the long grass in the back garden, Larry received a phone call from Detective Sergeant Simon Dawson, one of the officers who had questioned them after the discovery of the bones. DS Dawson informed Larry that the remains were that of a male in his early twenties. There was nothing in the remnants of his clothing to identify him but he was a smoker because they found a squashed packet of Senior Service cigarettes and a box of Swan Vesta matches in the residue of his trouser pockets. It was not possible to pinpoint an actual time of death but it was estimated that the deceased had been dead for approximately eighty years. It was also not possible to establish a cause of death but there did look to be a fracture to the skull and because of the whereabouts of the remains and the fact that the cellar had been sealed up, the coroner's verdict would have to be murder. He also added that there would be no further need to look in the cellar and that they were free to continue with the kitchen floor. Larry asked if they were likely to investigate the death further and was told they would look into it but not as a priority. It might be possible to identify the victim in due course but as the time of death most likely occurred during the Second World War, records would prove difficult. Furthermore, it was highly unlikely that the perpetrator was still living.

Chapter Four

On Monday morning, eager to hear the latest news, Denzil and Brett were back at Holly Cottage to commence work on the kitchen floor. Meanwhile, Larry and Kate having discussed the finding of the cellar in great detail had decided they wanted it left open and to have a new hinged trapdoor installed with tiles around it. Denzil, not surprised by their decision, rang a fellow tradesman who was a chippy and he agreed to make the trapdoor and its surround.

Shortly after they began work, Freddie, having been to the builders' merchants for materials, arrived to plaster the wall in the utility room; as he finished the job and they all stopped work for a tea break, Larry's mobile phone rang. It was Detective Sergeant Simon Dawson who told him that investigations had established that Holly Cottage along with the only other cottage situated in Lady Fern Lane had, prior to the end of the Second World War, belonged to Pengillirose Manor, now a hotel, for the occupation of its staff. Holly Cottage, was occupied by Archie Penrose, the estate's maintenance man, his wife Mavis and their two young children. Archie was killed in action during WW2 just before Christmas in 1942. After the war, the Pengillirose Estate, its land, manor house and both cottages were sold. The cottages were bought by a Peter Richardson who rented them out for a while and later sold Holly Cottage to a Thomas Mitchell. When the call ended, Larry repeated the police officer's news to Kate, Freddie, Denzil and Brett.

"Yes, I knew the cottages once belonged to the old Pengillirose Manor but had no idea who lived in them backalong," said Denzil, breaking a digestive biscuit in two, "but I suppose it stands to reason they'd have been for staff."

"And the body in the cellar can't be the maintenance man, Archie Penrose, who lived here if he was killed in 1942 during the war," mused Freddie, "so who on earth might it be?"

"Well, he can't be Peter Richardson either if he sold the place on to Thomas Mitchell." Kate frowned, "Actually it couldn't be him anyway, could it. Not if our mystery man died during the war, because Mr Richardson was obviously alive and well years later."

"The Thomas Mitchell, Simon mentioned must be the bloke you bought this place from but we all knew him as Tom," said Denzil, "Well, no, silly me, not Tom because the poor chap's dead, but you would have bought it from his widow."

"That's right," confirmed Larry, "we bought the house from a Mrs Elsie Mitchell."

"Going back to the remains," said Freddie, "whoever the bloke was, why wasn't he away at war? I mean, if as estimated he was in his early twenties, unless he was exempt, surely he would have been called up."

"I think we've found ourselves a little project," Kate spoke with enthusiasm, "because I don't know about you lot but I'm very keen to learn more and get to the bottom of this."

"Likewise." Larry addressed Denzil: "do you know much of the village's history?"

"Not really, even though I was born and bred here. As were my late parents and their parents before them. I've only lived out here in the Lane for the last two years. Before that I had a terraced house near the church. I know loads of people but not their history."

"In which case I think I know someone who'd be willing to do a bit of digging," said Freddie, with a twinkle in his eyes, "Two people in fact, if not three or even four."

Denzil chuckled. "Of course, Dilly, your lovely godmother. I should have thought of that."

"Who's your godmother?" Kate asked.

"Dilly, Dilly Granger. She's seventy-three years old, is as bright as a button and until she retired was a gym mistress in a girls' school up-country. She's been here for just over a year now and her closest friends are her next door neighbours, Amelia and Ernie Trewella, her gentleman friend, Orville King, and the vicar's housekeeper, Ivy Richards."

"And Dotty," Denzil added, "I often see Dilly and Dotty out jogging together."

Kate's jaw dropped. "She goes jogging at seventy-three?"

"Yes, she's keen to keep herself fit," Freddie acknowledged.

"So do your godmother and her friends know a lot about the village?" Larry asked.

"Not really," conceded Freddie, "but it's something that interests them. The previous owners of the house, Lavender Cottage, where my godmother lives has an interesting past as she and her friends, and me too for that matter, discovered when they looked into it, but I'll save telling you all about that for another day."

"Ivy's been in the village all her life so she knows a thing or two," Denzil added.

"True," agreed Freddie, "but she's only in her sixties so won't remember the war. Not that many people do now with it being so long ago."

"Well whatever it sounds fascinating, so before the place gets all dusty with the removal of the dividing wall, how about you bring them all round for a drink and a buffet on Wednesday evening and then we can chew over what we know," Kate eagerly suggested. "I'll knock something up because I do love cooking."

"Sounds lovely," said Freddie. "I know they'll be keen to meet you but there is a slight problem." Kate looked puzzled. Freddie chuckled. "I couldn't help but notice your cooker is disconnected from the mains and currently standing in the middle of the utility room."

"Oh bother, I didn't think of that and we can't get it back in here until the floor is finished."

"Not a problem anyway," said Freddie, "I'll suggest they all bring an offering of food and if I know them they'll bring bottles of booze too."

Larry rubbed his hands together. "Sounds great."

"Can I come too?" Brett asked. "I'm just as keen as you lot to know who the poor bloke was and what happened to him."

"Of course, the more the merrier and bring your girlfriend," said Kate. "You told me she's studying horticulture so I'd like to meet her as she might be able to give me some gardening advice."

"Brill! Thanks, yeah, she'll love that."

Freddie stood up. "And I'll bring my fiancée too, if that's okay."

"Please do. We're keen to get to know everyone as this is our forever home."

"Ideal. I could come up with a list of people who'd be keen to see what's going on here but we'll keep Wednesday simple and keep the gathering small. Meanwhile, I better get off and I'll call in to see my godmother on my way home so she can relay the news to her next door neighbours, plus Orville, and Ivy of course."

"Who's Ivy again?" Kate asked. "I know you said but can't remember."

"The vicar's housekeeper and a friend of my godmother. You'll like her. She's very amicable."

"Does she still read lavender tealeaves?" Denzil asked.

"No, she gave that up because no-one liked drinking it."

Kate pulled a face. "Yuck! Not surprised, it sounds ghastly."

Freddie chuckled. "It is but giving it up didn't put Ivy off dabbling with clairvoyance and what have you. According to Dilly, she's now studying fortune telling or some such nonsense with the aid of the internet would you believe."

Kate's jaw dropped. "Really! Now that might come in very useful while we're trying to find out what happened in the cellar."

Denzil smothered a smile. "I wouldn't bank on it, Kate."

Chapter Five

On Wednesday evening, Dilly, Orville, Amelia, Ernie and Ivy arrived together at Holly Cottage shortly after Denzil who was seated on a dining chair in the front sitting room talking to Larry. Kate greeted their guests as they entered the house and Denzil who knew both parties made the introductions.

"I've been doing a bit of investigating on your behalf," said Ivy, excitedly to Larry and Kate as she handed Kate a biscuit tin containing homemade sausage rolls, "which I think you'll find quite interesting, but I'll leave you in suspense for now and tell you about it when everyone else is here."

Kate's eyes shone. "Wonderful and thank you. I really look forward to hearing what you have to say."

While Orville placed two bottles of wine alongside other drinks on the window seat, Dilly handed Kate a broccoli and stilton quiche she had made. "She hasn't even told us what she's found out. Very secretive is our Ivy."

Kate's eyebrows rose. "Must be something interesting then. Anyway, while we wait for the rest to get here would you like to see around the place then I can point out what we're planning to do?" She laughed, "Oh dear, I make it sound as though we live in a stately home but as you can see it's anything but."

All five agreed they would very much like a look around the house but in the light of its recently discovered grisly secret and its lack of illumination they opted to give the cellar a miss.

When they returned indoors after finalising their tour with a wander around the overgrown back garden, they found that Brett and his girlfriend, Becky had also arrived. Unlike the older generation, Becky was keen to see inside the cellar and so Larry escorted her down the steps in the torchlight of his phone.

"I wonder what the poor chap you found looked like," she pondered on returning to the front room. "Because if we knew we'd be able to see if there was a likeness to anyone in the village now. I'd love to see a picture of him. Do you think he was once handsome?"

"No idea," chuckled Larry, "but he certainly wasn't very handsome when we found him."

Kate rolled her eyes and took Becky's arm. "Ignore him, love, and tell me a bit about yourself. Brett tells me you're into gardening."

"That'd right. I'm doing a course in horticulture at college and working part-time in a garden centre to earn some money. Of course we're on holiday from college now until September which is great as it gives me time to chill out."

"Well if you want a bit of extra company," said Kate, "our grandson, Jamie, and a friend of his hope to pop down sometime before they go back to school. If they do perhaps you could show them around the village. They're only thirteen so quite a bit younger than you but I think they'd prefer your company to being escorted out by their old grandparents."

"Love to. It's always nice to meet new people and I'm seventeen so they're not that much younger. What's more, I only work two days a week at the garden centre so I have plenty of spare time."

Dilly had listened with interest. "If and when you have a patch of the garden sorted, Kate, I've some wallflower plants you can have. I sowed the whole packet and swear every one germinated so I've far more than I'll ever need or have room for. They're not quite ready yet but when they are you're more than welcome to have some."

"Thank you, Dilly. Sounds wonderful. I love wallflowers, the scent reminds me of my childhood as they were one of Mum's favourite spring flowers."

At half past seven there was a knock on the front door. Kate answered to find Freddie on the doorstep with his fiancée, Max, a farmer who lived with her mother and Freddie at Hilltop Farm.

"Excellent, I think we're all here now so I'll plate up the buffet food and lay it out." Kate closed the door and directed Freddie and Max to join everyone else in the front sitting room where they were invited to help themselves to drinks.

Dilly watched their hostess lay out the food. When the last plate was placed on the table and Kate took her ease, she turned to Ivy. "So come on, spill the beans. I know you're longing to tell us what have you've found out."

Ivy took a seat at the table and placed her wineglass on a coaster. "Well, after you rang yesterday, Dilly, to tell me about tonight's lovely gathering and thank you, Kate and Larry for that, I gave a lot of thought to what we know so far, but of course I couldn't come up with anything useful because as you know I wasn't born till well after the war. Anyway, I decided to pop round and see Nora Rogers. At ninety-one she's the village's oldest inhabitant and has a razor sharp mind. What's more, she's lived here all her life and what she doesn't know isn't worth knowing."

Denzil chuckled. "And she can talk for England."

"She certainly can. Anyway, Nora remembers the Penrose family who lived here at Holly Cottage. And although she doesn't have many memories of Archie Penrose other than seeing him play the trumpet in the brass band at village fetes and hearing her dad rave about his skills as a batman for the local cricket team, she does remember their children. They had a couple, a girl and a boy, twins apparently, who thought their dad was really old because he was ten years older than their mum. Anyway, Nora used to play with the kids but when war broke out and Archie volunteered to join up, Mavis and the children went away up-country, Newbury, I think Nora said, to look after Mavis's mother who was in poor health. Needless to say the cottage was left empty and it stayed that way for several years because by the end of the war, poor Archie was dead and Mavis didn't want to come back here. Although I assume at some point she must have collected the remainder of their belongings but I don't suppose there would have been a great deal because Nora said the house was furnished by the Manor."

"Very interesting. Well done, Ivy," Larry was impressed.

"I agree, but do you know if poor Archie was killed overseas or if he was wounded and died back here from his injuries?" Kate asked.

"I know there are very few war graves here so I think, Archie most likely died and was buried overseas. If that's the case, having no grave to tend here might be another reason for Mavis having no desire to return. But whatever, Nora never saw any of the family again and eventually the house, and yours, as well, Denzil, were sold as was the Manor itself and quite a bit of land. It wasn't until sometime in the nineteen-fifties that Pete Richardson bought both places and converted the smallest bedrooms into bathrooms. He then put in tenants. Nora can't remember who first rented this place but whoever it was she doesn't think they were here very long because in 1962 Elsie Mitchell and her husband, Tom, who was a fireman, moved in here. Elsie of course being the lady you bought the house from."

"Who as we know," said Larry, "is now in a care home."

"That's right, she is. Been there just over a year now. She's a nice lady and her husband was too. Very sad. Poor man, he spent his working life doing a job he loved, helping others and then died shortly after he retired following a road traffic accident. Two cars were involved but Tom was not at fault. The other car was driving on the wrong side of the road."

"So roughly when was it that Tom died?" Kate asked.

"Around the turn of the century. The millennium one of course not the one before. I was in my early forties back then and remember it well. The attendance at the funeral was huge, and the flowers, well, I've never seen so many."

Dilly looked puzzled. "Going back a step if I may. Can I ask why I've never heard mention of ninety-one year old Nora before? It just seems odd that John, God rest his soul, never mentioned her when we were looking into the Bray family history last year."

Denzil answered. "It'd be because she was away for much of last autumn and winter. I believe it was Spain she went to. Somewhere warm anyway."

Ivy nodded. "Spot on Denzil. She went away with her sister who lives in St Austell and they stayed somewhere near Alicante. They went in September so about the same time as you moved here, Dilly, and came back in late February. So of course she wasn't here when John was helping look into the Bray family's history."

"Dear John," sighed Amelia, "I do miss him and this project would have been right up his street."

"Who's John?" asked Kate, keen to learn who everyone was.

"Sadly John is no longer with us," said Ernie, "but he was a retired fisherman who became our local historian and a very dear man he was too. His knowledge of the village, its inhabitants and its history were amazing, but I believe I'm right in saying his records, slides, pictures and so forth have all been passed on to the vicar."

"They have indeed," agreed Ivy. "John's brother, Bruce who inherited all John's stuff insisted the vicar take good care of it and maybe carry on John's good work, which the vicar has agreed to do."

"Really! He might be someone to visit then," said Larry, "the vicar, that is."

"And this lady, Nora, as well," added Kate.

Denzil finished his wine and placed the empty glass on the table. "I agree, but going back before the Mitchells to the Penroses who lived in this house. If they weren't here during the war years because Archie was fighting and Mavis was looking after her mum, then anyone could have dumped our mystery body in the cellar."

Larry topped up Denzil's glass. "It looks that way, yes."

"Does Nora recall anyone being unaccounted for back then?" Amelia asked, "I mean, if he was a local lad then surely someone would have reported him as missing."

"I didn't ask her that simply because I didn't want to overload her memory and I needed to digest and memorise all she'd said. So that's a question for another day."

"I'd love to meet her," enthused Dilly, "she sounds wonderful."

"So would I," said Amelia. Ernie agreed.

"You'll like her," said Freddie's fiancée, Max. "She was at school with my late granddad. He often mentioned her when reminiscing because she kept them all in order apparently."

Ivy smothered a smile. "She is remarkable and I've just remembered something else that she told me. Apparently when they were kids and this house stood empty they all reckoned it was haunted."

"Haunted!" Kate squealed, the look on her face, one of horror.

"Ernie chuckled. "Well, now I know that I can honestly say that I'm really glad we didn't have a poke around in your tomb-like cellar."

Chapter Six

On Thursday, Kate and Larry had the house to themselves. Denzil having said the previous evening that he and Brett would return on Friday morning to fit the trapdoor which by then should be ready. Once installed they would finish laying the floor but to minimise disruption they would leave the removal of the dividing wall until kitchen fitters had installed the new units.

To make use of their time, Larry renewed the wiring in the cellar and fitted a fluorescent light from the beams. Then, with not much enthusiasm, he cleared the area out and swept the floor. Rusty tools which he thought could be restored to their former glory and made useful, he took into the utility room to work on at a later date. Kate meanwhile, eager to feel the warm sun on her face, went out into the back garden to dig over a flower bed, the outline of which was just visible amongst the weeds due to its granite stone edging. As she removed the weeds and threw them into a heap, a robin appeared and watched from the lower branch of a rhododendron from where he occasionally swooped for a tasty morsel unearthed by her digging.

When the bed was cleared, Kate stood back with a feeling of satisfaction. The area would be ideal for the wallflower plants Dilly had mentioned and she would fill in the gaps with spring bulbs.

Before putting away her tools she contemplated clearing another overgrown bed alongside the boundary fence adjoining farmland. Little seemed to grow in the border other than an abundance of Japanese Anemones, a large, flourishing hydrangea, weeds and a wild fuchsia. Feeling a slight ache in her back she decided not to over exert herself and leave it for another day.

Just after ten on Friday morning, Kate left Denzil and Brett to finish the kitchen floor and fit the trapdoor. Larry likewise was busy but in the utility room where he was improving the lighting before taking a trip to the shops for groceries. With a spring in her step Kate walked along Lady Fern Lane and into the village where as pre-arranged she met up with Ivy, Dilly and Amelia: their purpose to visit the village news veteran, Nora Rogers.

Nora lived in the heart of Trenwalloe Sands two doors up from the post office in Smugglers Lane. Her granite-built, semi-detached house had a small front garden with a central cobbled path leading from the wooden gate to the door. Before they had a chance to knock, the door swung open.

"Hello and welcome. It's lovely to have visitors and I've been watching out for you," she took Kate's hand, "and going by Ivy's description you must be the new owner of the cottage in Lady Fern Lane. A beautiful location although a little too isolated for me."

Kate smiled, wondering how Ivy had described her. "That's why we love it. Such a contrast to living in a city as we did for many years. Anyway, I'm delighted to meet you, Nora."

"And I'm delighted to meet you too." Nora turned to Dilly and Amelia, "and you two ladies must be from what we used to know as the Square."

"We are," said Dilly. They introduced themselves.

"Wonderful. I've heard all about you and your antics from various sources." She stepped back to allow them to enter the hallway, "and of course it's lovely to see you too, Ivy. Come on in all of you and make yourselves at home while I get the kettle on."

Nora, a slight figure, led the way into the kitchen like a woman thirty years her junior. The kettle was on and mugs taken from a cupboard before her visitors had a chance to take seats around the kitchen table.

"Lovely room," said Kate, admiringly, "and what a view."

"It is, I agree and for that reason I spend much of my day in here reading and doing crossword puzzles." She pointed to an armchair in the corner of the room where lay a Pembroke Welsh Corgi watching through half closed eyes, "That's when Reginald Rex will permit me use of my favourite chair."

"Reginald Rex Rogers," chuckled Amelia, "What a lovely name."

"Yes, I'm a sucker for alliteration. Probably why I was so fond of the erstwhile landlord of the Duck and Parrot."

"Would that be before Gail and Robert Stevens took over or are you going back further than that?" Dilly asked.

"Before Gail and Robert. Duke's a dear man, he's retired now and lives in one of the bungalows on the Buttercup Field Estate."

"Duke, I vaguely remember him," said Amelia, "he left the pub shortly after we, that is my husband Ernie and I, moved here but I can't remember what he looked like and I wouldn't have remembered he was called Duke."

"Well, that's what he's known as but his full name is Marmaduke Mapplebeck," chuckled Nora, "and a fine looking man he is too."

"And a real good egg," said Ivy, "We thought when he left the pub he might leave the village so we were thrilled when he decided to settle here. Having said that, we don't see much of him now because he suffers with a bad back and puts it down to rolling around barrels and being on his feet all day for the best part of his life."

When tea was made and biscuits, sugar and milk placed on the table, Nora pulled out a dining chair and sat down with her guests. "Now, which part of memory lane would you like me to totter down today?"

Dilly smiled at the image of Nora's petite frame tottering down a lane with Reginald Rex at her heels. "We're hoping you can recall if during the war any young man from the village was reported missing."

Ivy stirred a spoonful of sugar into her tea. "Yes, because we're dying to find out who the poor chap in the cellar might be but at the moment we don't have a clue."

"Funny you should ask that because after you'd gone the other day, Ivy, I put my thinking cap on to see if I could come up with a name and the only one was Harold Jenkins. The Jenkins' family ran the pub at the time and Harold was their son. Needless to say he was called up soon after war broke out and was conscripted to serve in the Army. I remember there was a lot of gossip when he came home on leave and then just disappeared into thin air. Wagging tongues reckoned he'd done a runner. Deserted because he didn't want to go back. Others though said that was nonsense. He liked the Army and wished he'd joined when he left school and before war had broken out. Of course it all went right over my head. I was more interested in climbing trees," she chuckled, "I was a bit of a tomboy."

"So when would that be?" Ivy asked, "When he disappeared, I mean."

"Hmm, I suppose I'd have been about eleven at the time. Yes of course I was and it was September, my birthday month. September 1943, but I don't know the exact date."

"And was he never seen again?" Amelia asked.

"Nope, and for that reason as soon as the war ended the Jenkins family left the pub and moved to somewhere in Dorset. I think they believed there might have been a grain of truth in the gossip and were ashamed. But I don't know and I was too young then to form an opinion. I know Mum liked Harold though and she said he was no coward."

"Might he not have turned up in the years after the war to see his parents in Dorset having found out by some means that they had moved there?" Amelia asked.

"Yes, it's possible I suppose. But back then before the internet it would have been much trickier to establish his parents' whereabouts without speaking to someone from the village."

Ivy chuckled. "And had he come back here making enquiries it wouldn't have taken long for the whole village to have heard about it."

"Very true." Nora reached for a biscuit and broke it in two. "Back then when there was less traffic and people chatted to their neighbours out in the street and over garden walls, there was not much went on that one and all didn't get to know about."

"Did he by any chance have any brothers or sisters?" Dilly asked, "This Harold, I mean."

"A sister. I'm sure he had a sister. Yes, of course he did, she was a pretty young thing and helped out in the pub. And if I remember correctly she was engaged to someone in the Forces. Whether or not she married him though, I've no idea. As I said, the family left the village after the war and I'm pretty sure she went with them."

"I don't suppose you remember her name, do you?" Dilly crossed her fingers.

Nora closed her eyes and slowly went through letters of the alphabet. "G, I'm sure her name began with a G." Her mouth formed different sounds and when she reached Gr she squealed with delight. "Grace. Of course, yes, her name was Grace."

Dilly excitedly clapped her hands. "Wonderful. Now if we can track her down she might be able to tell us a bit about her brother."

Amelia smiled. "I think you're being a bit optimistic there. If Grace was working in the pub during the war she'd be a hundred or more now. Assuming she was born in the early nineteen-twenties, that is."

"Oh bother!" Dilly felt deflated.

"Don't be too disheartened," said Nora, "I mean, she may have had children and if so they might know a bit of the family's history."

"True," agreed Amelia, "and I don't want to be a wet blanket, but Grace's descendants won't be easy to find if she married and changed her name."

"Oh dear," Dilly groaned. "We don't seem to be getting far and at the moment we don't even know if the poor bloke we found is Harold Jenkins."

"No," said Nora, "but let's be positive because if you can find some of Grace's living relatives, the police would be able to do a DNA thingy and then we'll know one way or another."

Having completed his chores, Larry arrived back at Holly Cottage with the groceries shortly after Kate had arrived home and was in the process of making tea for Denzil and Brett. Inside the cupboard beneath the stairs, the new trapdoor was in situ and the last floor tiles having been laid, were ready for grouting.

Larry placed the bags of groceries on the draining board and nodded his head with approval. "The floor looks smashing, lads, even before the grouting's done." He stepped into the cupboard and lifted the new trap door. "A perfect fit. I really feel we're getting somewhere now."

"Well we'll have the grouting done in no time and then we'll be out of your hair for a couple of days while you get the kitchen fitted," said Denzil.

Kate glanced at the calendar. "And that's on Monday. The kitchen fitters being here, I mean. And they reckon it's quite straight forward so it should all be done in a day."

"Ideal. In which case we'll be back on Wednesday and that'll give you a chance to move stuff around in the two sitting rooms so we can get to the wall."

"Excellent." Kate lifted the tray of mugs and carried it out to the front sitting room. Over tea and biscuits, she then repeated to three pairs of enthusiastic ears all they had learned from Nora.

Meanwhile, Amelia, Dilly and Ivy, eager to digest and discuss Nora's information, made their way to Lavender Cottage. No sooner had Dilly switched on the kettle than there was a knock on the door.

"I'll go," Amelia jumped up, answered the door and returned with Dotty Gibson looking nicely tanned.

"Ah, you're back, Dotty. Did you have a nice holiday?" Dilly took another mug from the kitchen cabinet and dropped in a teabag as Dotty took a seat.

"Yes, it was brilliant, thanks and we got back late last night. The weather was absolutely glorious. We had a fantastic time and the rest has done Gerry the power of good." She leaned forwards in her chair, "But what's all this I hear about a body in the cellar at Holly Cottage?"

"You didn't waste any time finding that out," said Ivy, "if you only got back last night."

"Ah well, that's the beauty of having a boyfriend in the police force. Gerry went back to work this morning and rang me a few minutes ago. Knowing where to come for the latest news I headed straight round here."

In her early forties, Dotty, a divorcee and writer of romantic fiction, whose hobbies were blogging about fitness and health issues, and jogging, was also renowned for her liking of gossip. She lived alone in Short Lane where her house overlooked Trenwalloe Sands. Her boyfriend, Police Sergeant, Gerry Freeman also lived alone but in the heart of the village near to the pub.

"Well, fancy that," said Dotty, after the ladies had filled her in with the details, "when I saw them moving in little did I know their arrival would bring a bit of excitement to the village."

Ivy placed her empty tea mug on the floor by her feet. "You saw them moving in? I didn't know that."

"Yes, it was the day before Gerry and I went on holiday and I was out jogging." Dotty patted her flat stomach, "I need to get running again pretty quick because as you can see I put on a few pounds while we were away. Having said that, I've plenty of time so I think I'll leave it until tomorrow and go for an extra-long run out Lady Fern way and call in to introduce myself at the same time. You see, I didn't see them on the day they moved in, Ivy. I only saw the removal van."

"That's right, I remember you telling me that," agreed Amelia, "I'd forgotten all about it though. You passed on the news to me when I saw you shortly after your jog when I came out the post office."

Dotty clasped her hands in a prayer like manner. "I do hope you'll let me help with your investigations. I mean, after looking into the Bray family's past we're almost experts, aren't we? Cold case experts, that is. Although I suppose since this is a new case it's not a cold case, is it? Anyway, whatever, I'll be able to get Robin to help us too. At least, I might be able to. I've not met him yet, you see, but Gerry assures me we'll get on like a house on fire because he writes too, crime novels to be precise. You know, detective type things. I've not read any of his books though and perhaps I should before he gets here. I'll see if Gerry has any of his work because I know he likes reading."

Dilly cast her eyes towards Amelia and Ivy who looked as nonplussed as she felt. "You've lost us, Dotty. We've no idea who Robin is."

"Oh sorry, yes. He's a friend of Gerry's and also a copper. Well actually, he's not a copper now because he left the Force a couple of years ago after he was badly injured in a road traffic accident. He's fine now though but has a limp. Gerry and Robin have known each other for years. They met at Hendon when they joined the Force and have always kept in touch. Anyway, Robin was due to go away with his girlfriend tomorrow but since the holiday was arranged some time ago they've parted company and his ex is now going to take someone else in his place. Robin, feeling he'd like to get away too for a change of scenery, rang Gerry last night as we were leaving for the airport to see if he could come and visit him for a week or so and then while he's here, pop down to Penzance to see an aunt who he's not seen for ages. Gerry was delighted, said yes and Robin should be here tomorrow. Of course Gerry will have to work while Robin's here because he's used up all his holiday, so I shall be taking him under my wing, so to speak."

Amelia's eyes shone. "A crime writer! Now, that could be very useful."

"I agree," enthused Dilly, "and an ex copper too. What's more, I like the name Robin. It reminds me of the little bird."

"Actually, his name's not Robin, it's Oliver but everyone calls him Robin. It's because of his surname. It's Hood, you see." Dotty chuckled as three pairs of eyes rolled. "Anyway, that's enough about Robin. Tell me everything you can about the Greenwoods because I'm longing to meet them."

Chapter Seven

On Tuesday morning, Kate and Larry carried small items of furniture from the two sitting rooms into the empty hallway and returned the kitchen table and chairs to their allotted place in the corner of the refurbished kitchen. Larger pieces of furniture they left in the two rooms, grouped them together and covered all items with old sheets. When done, everything was ready for Denzil and Brett to remove the dividing wall the next day.

In the early evening, feeling tired after her physical labour, and mental exertion following a visit from a very talkative Dotty, Kate suggested to Larry that they visit the pub for a drink and to save them cooking have something to eat as well. Larry thought it an excellent idea; he was keen to get acquainted with his new local and its licensees and there was always the chance that Gail and Robert Stevens might know something of the wartime licensees albeit a long time ago.

The Duck and Parrot stood on the sea front along the main road. To reach it from Lady Fern Lane, the Greenwoods walked along Back Lane, into Manor Road and then Church Street where the church overlooked the village green. Opposite the church was the vicarage. Only glimpses of the roof were visible from the road; the rest of the house was masked by trees and large shrubs.

The village green, laid mainly to grass and shaded by trees was a popular meeting place for locals. Small flower beds tended by a group of volunteers, were separated by gravel paths and interspersed with wooden benches. In the centre stood three fruit trees; an apple, a pear and a plum, the fruits of which locals were encouraged to pick. As Kate and Larry walked along the gravel paths they came to a war memorial and amongst the list of names saw that of Archie Henry Penrose, one time maintenance man at the old manor who had lived at Holly Cottage along with his wife, Mavis and their two children.

Kate shuddered. “That’s so sad because seeing his name makes him seem more real, if you know what I mean.”

“It does, and it’s just occurred to me that Holly Cottage lost one of its householders, Archie Penrose in World War Two and then later retired fireman Tom Mitchell, husband of the lady in the care home we bought the cottage from. Tom died following a road traffic accident and now we’ve found the remains of some bloke yet to be formally identified in our cellar. I hope that doesn’t mean our house is jinxed.”

“Don’t say that. Especially on top of rumours that it’s haunted.”

“Hmm, no comment,” Larry then read through the rest of the names on the memorial. “It’s just a thought, but I wonder if any of these other people listed had connections to, or were even friends with, our missing Harold Jenkins. That’s if it is him we found.”

“I expect they all knew each other. The village would no doubt have been much smaller back then as most of the houses seem to be post-war.”

The pub was busy inside with drinkers propping up the bar, while outside families sat around tables enjoying the early evening sun as their children amused themselves in the play area. A few of the families were locals but most were holiday makers relaxing with a drink during the summer break.

Kate and Larry were greeted at the bar by Robert Stevens. As they bought drinks and ordered food, Larry asked Robert if he knew anything of the pub’s previous licensees and during the nineteen-forties in particular.

"No, sorry. Unfortunately I can't go back any further than Marmaduke Mapplebeck, my predecessor. But if anyone knows it'll be him because he was here for quite a number of years and we often get people, holiday makers in particular, asking after him."

"Perhaps we ought to pay him a visit then. Do you know where he's living now?"

"He's definitely somewhere on the Buttercup Field Estate and I think he has one of the bungalows but I don't know which one."

Kate nodded. "Yes, I remember Nora saying he'd moved up there. We're new to the village though so have no idea where the estate is."

"Ah, it's easy enough to find." Robert gave them directions. Larry thanked him and as they picked up their drinks, the landlord wished them well before moving on to serve someone waving an empty pint glass.

Not wanting to be indoors they took their drinks out into the beer garden. "I think you'd better give Ivy, Dilly or Amelia a ring and arrange a visit with them to see this Marmaduke chap," said Larry, as they sat at one of the picnic tables.

"Yes, you're right so I'll ring Ivy in the morning. She's been here the longest, all her life in fact, and she knows Marmaduke because she spoke fondly of him. With any luck we'll be able to go tomorrow."

After they had eaten, both agreed they were full and didn't want another drink. So just before eight they set off for home. Shortly after they left the premises, Dotty and Gerry entered the bar with Gerry's guest, ex-police officer, Oliver Hood, known as Robin. No sooner had the three bought their drinks than Freddie arrived with his fiancée, Max.

"Hey, come and join us." Dotty stood and beckoned the newly arrived couple to their table. "You must meet Gerry's old friend, Robin." She turned to Robin, "this is my dear friend Max and her fiancé, Freddie who I was telling you about on our way here."

After introductions were made and Freddie bought drinks for himself and Max, Dotty explained how she hoped Robin, with time on his hands, might be able to shed some light on the discovery of the body in the cellar. "Not," she concluded, "that we can do a great deal until we know who he is, or should I say, was."

"It certainly would help if we had a name," agreed Robin, "Anyway, I'm happy to do what I can. I was going to pass the time doing a bit of research for my next book and what have you but that can wait."

"So how many books have you written?" Max asked.

"Twelve. Six in a series and six standalones."

"And do you sell enough to make a living?"

Robin laughed. "How I'd like to say yes but that would be a gross exaggeration. I make a bit, and when I bring out a new book sales are quite good. To pay the bills though I work part-time on the bar in our local pub. I enjoy it as it gives me a chance to observe people: a necessity when forming characters in one's mind."

"Fascinating. I shall get one of your books to read on my Kindle."

To Max's surprise Robin blushed. "That's kind of you but let's change the subject. I hate talking about myself even though it was me who brought the subject of books up." He looked from Freddie to Max, "Dotty tells me you two are getting married later this year and that you're a farmer, Max."

Max beamed. "That's right, I am and we are."

"So when's the wedding and where's the farm?"

"The wedding is to be in December and the farm, Hilltop Farm, is just outside the village. It's been in the family for quite a few years and when Dad died I took it over."

"You don't look a bit like a farmer."

Max laughed. "And just what should a farmer look like?"

"Well, umm, yes, let's talk about the wedding. A winter wedding. Sounds rather nice and you might even get snow for confetti."

"Now that would be lovely but I think it unlikely. Winters are mild down here so we're more likely to get rain."

Dotty tipped the remains of her bottle of tonic water onto her gin. "Talking of weddings. Do you think Orville will ever get your godmother to marry him, Freddie? They make a really sweet pair."

"Oh, I'm sure he'll succeed in the end. Orville is very tenacious and there's no doubt about the fact there's a sparkle in Dilly's eyes whenever they're together."

On Wednesday morning, Kate tried to ring Ivy after breakfast but the call went to voicemail. Not one to be deterred she rang Dilly and told her of their meeting with pub landlord, Robert, and how sadly he had not been able to help with details of the wartime licensees. He had, however, suggested they visit his predecessor, Marmaduke Mapplebeck. Dilly greeted the proposal with enthusiasm and said she'd ring round to see if anyone else would like to pay the pub's erstwhile landlord a visit.

Twenty minutes later, Dilly returned Kate's call to say she and Amelia would accompany Kate to visit Marmaduke. She had managed to contact Ivy who would have gone along as well but it was her day to take Nora on a weekly shopping trip to the supermarket. She added that Ivy had been driving when Kate tried to ring her hence she had been unable to answer her phone. Dilly also mentioned she had contacted Orville who lived on the Buttercup Field Estate and who knew where Marmaduke lived but he wasn't sure of the number. Apparently it was either five or seven, whichever one had a blue door.

"Do you think we ought to ring Marmaduke first to see if it's okay for us to visit?" Kate asked.

"Amelia suggested that but it appears no-one knows his mobile number and he isn't in the telephone directory. So we assume he doesn't have a landline."

"Oh well, never mind. If he's not in or if it's inconvenient, we'll try again another day."

Kate slipped her mobile phone into her pocket, delighted to have a reason to leave the house. For Denzil and Brett had arrived to remove the dividing wall with Larry's help and she was keen to get away from the dust the demolition would inevitably create.

Dilly and Amelia met up with Kate at the entrance to the Buttercup Field Estate and made their way along the curved pavement looking out for numbers five and seven. It was number seven that had a blue door. Timorously, Kate knocked. The door was answered by a tall man with thick, wavy, white hair. He looked distinguished, was extremely handsome and had a welcoming smile. Because Nora had described Marmaduke Mapplebeck as a fine looking man, all were confident they were at the correct address. After introducing themselves and asking if he knew anything of the Duck and Parrot's previous licensees especially during the early forties, Marmaduke, intrigued by the question, invited them in.

"As a matter of fact I do know a bit from back then and that's because during my last summer at the boozer a retired couple called in and asked if they could have a look round. The reason they said was because the female's grandparents ran the pub once upon a time."

"Really! I suppose it'd be too much to expect you to remember her name," Dilly crossed her fingers.

A broad grin spread across Marmaduke's face. "You meet a lot of people in the pub trade so normally I'd say I've not the foggiest idea but in this case I do remember her name. The reason being I'm a sucker for alliteration."

"Like Nora," chuckled Amelia.

"You've met Nora then. Smashing lady, she's a breath of fresh air."

"And amazing for her age," Amelia added.

"She is that."

"So, what was her name?" Dilly eagerly asked, "I'm referring of course to the lady who called in and asked to have a look around the pub."

"Sophie Sally Sackitt. A real tongue twister, isn't it? Of course she wasn't born a Sackitt; that was her married name and I've no idea what her maiden name was. Anyway, when I told her my name she laughed. I then asked her when her grandparents had the pub and she said before and during the Second World War and that her mother was in the Women's Land Army and also helped in the pub. Apparently the family left after the war. Anyway, I showed her round and she was quite fascinated and took a few pictures."

Kate was overwhelmed. "She has to be Grace's daughter then. I've gone all goose-pimply."

"Likewise," Dilly couldn't wipe the smile from her face.

Marmaduke steepled his fingers. "So would I be being nosy if I asked why you want to know?"

"Sorry, we should have said." Kate then explained about the discovery of a long deceased body in the cellar of her new home in Lady Fern Lane and how there was a chance the remains were that of Harold Jenkins, son of the then licensees of the Duck and Parrot who disappeared while home on leave during the war.

"Ah yes, I heard something about some old bones being found but can't remember who told me. Not the best way to be welcomed to a new home though, is it."

"No, maybe not but it's certainly given us something to think about and it's also enabled us to make new friends and probably a lot quicker than if we'd not found the poor bloke."

They stayed for another hour during which Marmaduke made them mugs of tea and they chatted about the village and its inhabitants. Then just before lunch, they thanked Marmaduke for his help and eager to look on social media with high hopes of finding a Sophie Sally Sackitt, they hurried back to Lavender Cottage. While Dilly made mugs of coffee and sliced up a gooey chocolate cake, Kate searched for Sophie's name on Facebook. Suddenly she squealed with delight. "How lucky is that! I think I've found her." She turned her phone to face Dilly and Amelia on which a happy looking elderly lady was displayed on the small screen.

"What does it say about her?" Dilly asked.

"Not a great deal but she lives in Surrey and was born in 1950."

"It has to be her," said Amelia. "You must send her a message, Kate."

"Okay, but what shall I say?"

"For now just ask if her mother was called Grace and if she had a brother called Harold Jenkins and tell her that you'll explain why you've asked if the answer is positive." Amelia raised her fingers. "Oh, and mention Cornwall too, but perhaps not the pub."

Kate arrived back at Holly Cottage to find the wall had been removed and Larry was outside the open back door piling up dry, dusty lathes beside a heap of plaster chunks.

"Brilliant, you're back. Come and see this." Larry shook dust from his hands and led Kate back inside where from the floor he picked up a lump of plaster. "Before we demolished the wall we tore off some of the loose wallpaper and we found this underneath." Larry handed the plaster to Kate. Scrawled on discoloured green paint, inside a heart shape was the declaration - *SC loves AN*.

"Wow! This is fantastic. A real piece of history but who are SC and AN?"

"No idea but more to the point, did they have anything to do with Harold's death?"

"Well, I don't see why they would have but it might be a clue. Do the initials mean anything to Denzil?"

"Sadly not and we all agreed they could refer to anyone from any age. They obviously weren't written by Mavis and Archie Penrose though or for that matter by Elsie and Tom Mitchell."

"Well it's no good me wracking my brains because like you I don't know the names of the village's past residents." Kate turned the plaster over in her hand. "This I think is one for Nora."

In the early evening as Kate and Larry cleared away the last of the dust and vacuumed the carpet in the hallway, Kate's phone buzzed with a message from Sophie Sackitt to say that her grandparents were called Jenkins and they had a son called Harold who was the brother of her mother Grace. Harold was also her uncle but she never knew him because he went missing during the war. She also added that the family lived in Cornwall where they ran a pub.

Feeling that news concerning the probable fate of Sophie's Uncle Harold should be relayed to her by the police and not themselves, Larry rang Detective Sergeant Simon Dawson and told him they might have found a match. DS Dawson thanked him and said they would contact the lady in question and follow it up.

Chapter Eight

After a restless night's sleep, Larry woke up on Thursday morning in a cold sweat. He had been dreaming. Dreaming that he was lying in a cellar unable to move but aware of someone at the top of the steps stacking bricks. When he told Kate, she laughed. "Well it won't take much working out as to what triggered that, will it?"

"No, I suppose not but it was horrible and so real at the time."

"Dreams usually are. Come on, time to get up. There's lots to do and our trusty tradesmen will be here soon."

When Denzil and Brett arrived to continue work, Larry told them about his dream and Denzil was as unsympathetic as Kate. "I don't suppose you got to see the face of the chap with the bricks, did you? Be great if you did as it'd help us track him down."

"Well, no, and I couldn't so much see him as hear him. It was all very muzzy."

"Probably the ghost of the dead bloke putting ideas in your head," teased Kate.

"Ghost?" Larry looked shocked.

"Hmm, remember, Ivy told us that Nora reckoned this place was haunted."

"Poppycock," spluttered Larry, "you know full well, Kate, that I don't believe in that sort of nonsense."

"Well, I'm not sure that I do either but I wish we'd got her to tell us more about it when we went to see her the other day. As it is, I never gave it a thought. She and whoever her mates were must have a reason to make such a claim though so I must ask her about it next time I see her."

"Well why don't you pop along and see her now," suggested Larry, "not that I want to hear any more on the subject."

"I'll give Ivy a ring and see if she can arrange it. We need to see Nora anyway to see if she can shed any light on the initials you found on the wall."

Kate phoned her new friend who shortly after rang back to say a meeting would not possible that day because the local Darby and Joan Club of which Nora was a member were booked to go on an outing to one of the National Trust properties. However, Nora would give Ivy a ring in due course to arrange a visit at a later date.

Kate felt deflated. "Oh well, never mind, I suppose I can make myself useful here."

"Yep," agreed Larry. "Now the sun's shining it shows there are films of dust on just about everything."

Kate groaned. "Okay, I'll deal with the dust but first I must ring Dilly and tell her of the initials you found so that she and the others can ask around. I should have mentioned it to Ivy just now but never gave it a thought."

As Kate picked up her phone, Denzil stepped into the hallway with tools he'd collected from his van. "Before I forget. Is there any more news about the lady you hoped would be related to poor old Harold? You know, the one you told me about when you got back from seeing Marmaduke. You said she lived in Surrey and you'd messaged her."

Kate's eyes shone. "Yes, there is, Denzil, and I'm pleased to say we have a match. Her name's Sophie and she messaged back last night to say her mother was called Grace and her maiden name was Jenkins. What's more, Grace had a brother called Harold and their parents ran a pub in Cornwall. After we'd read and digested the message, Larry rang the police and spoke to DS Dawson who rang back late last night to say the Surrey police had been informed and would be seeing Sophie this morning to explain the situation here and hopefully they'll be able to take a DNA sample. We have our fingers well and truly crossed."

"Well done. You're making good progress."

After she had phoned Dilly and before she began to dust, Kate went into the back part of the newly created big room. "Will I be in your way, Denzil, if I pull off wallpaper from the walls not affected by your work? It's just I'm curious to know if there might be any more initials under there."

"Funny you should say that because I had wondered myself, but no, feel free. We'll be working in the middle so if you want to start over by the window we'll be out of each other's way."

Most of the wallpaper came away with ease due to it getting damp when the property was unoccupied during the winter months. But there were still places where Kate had to dampen the paper to loosen it. The end wall around the window revealed nothing. However, as she neared the centre of the room where the now demolished wall had once stood, she caught sight of a capital G written in pencil. With a squeal of delight she scraped away at the paper; Larry, Denzil and Brett already by her side. Within minutes she revealed the words *I love Georgie*. Excited by her find, Kate took a picture on her phone and forwarded it to her fellow investigators with a message of explanation.

During breakfast a few days later, Kate's mobile phone rang, it was their thirteen year old grandson, Jamie, asking if the offer still stood for himself and his best friend, Mike, to come and stay for a week or two before they went back to school in September; a subject mentioned backalong when Larry and Kate first told of their intended move to Cornwall.

Jamie lived with his parents on the outskirts of Bristol. Mike was Jamie's best friend and they had known each other since pre-school days. Kate told Jamie they'd be delighted to have them to stay and both spare rooms were ready and waiting for whenever they chose to make the journey. Jamie thanked his grandmother and said they hoped to be down some time during the following week and would confirm the exact date once their parents had arranged train tickets.

No sooner had Kate finished the call than Larry's phone rang. It was DS Dawson with the latest news. He told Larry that as previously mentioned, Surrey police had visited Sophie Sally Sackitt, Harold Jenkins's niece, and DNA was taken that same day. They had now received the results which confirmed the identity of the body in the cellar as that of Harold Jenkins, son of the then licensees. He added that at Mrs Sackitt's request the remains were to be cremated and she would then collect the ashes and arrange for their burial near to his parents in Dorset. She had also asked if it would be possible to meet up with the owners of Holly Cottage in order to see where her uncle had been found. Larry said that was not a problem and asked the DS to pass his condolences to Mrs Sackitt along with his phone number to enable them to arrange a meeting at her convenience.

As Larry ended his call, Kate's mobile phone rang again.

"Goodness me, we are popular this Tuesday morning." Kate answered her phone. The caller was Ivy to say she'd spoken to Nora, and Nora said they'd be welcome to call in anytime and the reason she'd not been in touch before was because she had caught a bit of a cold while on the Darby and Joan outing and didn't want to spread germs. Kate expressed her sympathy and then rang Dilly whereupon they arranged to meet up along with Amelia and Ivy at two o'clock outside the church on the village green. They would then walk along to Nora's together.

"How's the building work going?" Dilly asked, as Kate jumped up from the bench where she had waited.

"Nearly finished, at least the muckiest part is done now. Your Freddie just has to make good the walls and ceiling and Denzil has yet to get the French doors fitted. After that we can paint the walls, get a carpet down and the room will be back in use."

"And are you pleased with it?" Amelia asked.

"Oh yes. We love it. Denzil said it would bring in more light having windows either end of the now big room but it's even brighter than we'd imagined. And you should see the French doors. They only arrived yesterday and they're absolutely gorgeous. Denzil's fitting them today so they should be in place by the time I get home. Then we just need to decide whether we want them to lead out onto a patio or whether to go the whole hog and have a conservatory."

"That's a tricky one," said Ivy. "My sister has a conservatory but says it's too hot in there in the summer and too cold in the winter. She's got central heating and has thought of getting a radiator put out there. Don't know whether she will though. She lives alone so there doesn't seem much point."

As they turned into Smugglers' Lane they spotted Nora waving to them from her doorstep. On reaching her house she greeted them with the same enthusiasm as on their previous visit. "I've heard on the grapevine that it's been confirmed that the poor chap you found is Harold Jenkins. Is that right?"

Kate was astonished. "My goodness, news does travel fast around here. We only found out ourselves this morning."

Ivy nodded to the neighbouring house. "Young Brett lives there with his parents so I expect he messaged them as soon as he heard."

Kate chuckled. "And Brett's parents told you, Nora."

"Spot on. Jill, Brett's mum, is a treasure and always willing to share village news. Anyway, come on in and we'll get the kettle on. Because I thought you might pop round today I made a batch of rock buns. Not something I do very often nowadays."

When mugs of tea were empty and all the rock buns eaten, Kate told the ladies about Larry's dream and her suggestion that it might be the Holly Cottage ghost putting thoughts into his head.

Dilly laughed. "I knew the ghost is what you wanted to ask Nora about but didn't know the reason why."

Nora looked over her shoulder as though to check they weren't to be overheard, "Oh, but we really did think the house was haunted when we were young. In fact we even went inside to have a look around for ourselves. You see, the Penroses, who as you know had tenancy back then, used to leave a key to the back door under a stone beneath the kitchen window. Not sure why they bothered to lock up at all because everyone knew where the key was. Anyway, we, I think there were about half a dozen of us, went in because some old boy reckoned he'd heard weird noises coming from inside when out walking his dog one evening. He knew it couldn't be Archie or Mavis because Mavis and the children were up-country and by then poor old Archie had been killed. Anyway, the chap whoever he was, with the dog didn't investigate because it was already getting dark. We all reckoned he was too scared though." Nora chuckled, "Being kids with over active imaginations we all thought the ghost might have been Archie." She shuddered, "Oh, I can still remember that feeling. The house was really cold even though it was summer and it was dark in there too. At least it was in the kitchen where the blackout curtains were pulled together. Needless to say we didn't see any celestial beings but it felt like there was something there and after a few minutes we ran out, all having scared the living daylights out of each other."

"That's interesting," said Amelia, "because if everyone knew where the back door key was kept, then whoever sealed up the cellar with poor Harold in it would have had no problem getting into the house."

"Very true, so when was this, Nora?" asked Dilly, "I mean, if it's around the time Harold went missing then it's possible the noises the old boy with the dog heard could have been because someone was in there sealing up the cellar."

Nora gasped. "Goodness me, yes. It would have been September 1943 because when we went to explore I was wearing a bracelet I'd had for my eleventh birthday and was scared I might lose it in the dark. It was a bit loose, you see, because I was a skinny thing back then. Well, I'm not very big now. Anyway, you're probably right. Damn, because if that's the case it means the place wasn't and isn't haunted at all."

"Well, seeing as I live there, that's a relief and I know Larry will be pleased too." Kate then lifted up the bag she had brought with her and took out the piece of plaster. "Meanwhile, perhaps you'd look at this Nora and tell us if the initials mean anything to you."

Nora took the plaster. "Where did you get this?"

"From the wall Denzil and Brett removed to knock our two sitting rooms into one. It was under several layers of wallpaper."

"Really!" Nora closed her eyes, deep in thought. "SC loves AN. Oh dear, nothing springs to mind and it'd help if we knew when it was written because I've known quite a few people come and go over the years."

Dilly chuckled, "Yes, very remiss of them not to have included the date."

"Well whatever, it must be a few years ago if it was beneath several layers of wallpaper," reasoned Amelia, "and it can't be anyone who lived there because people don't write on their own walls. Having said that, someone might have scribbled it before they hung the wallpaper. But then we've already established the initials don't tally with either the Penroses or the Mitchells, so that can't be the case."

"No, they don't," agreed Ivy, "but I think I'm right in saying that Pete Richardson who bought the two houses in Lady Fern Lane when they and the Manor house were sold, rented them out after he'd installed bathrooms. So it's possible the initials belong to whoever the tenants were between him buying the place and the Penroses moving in."

"Ouch," groaned Dilly, "this is getting complicated."

"I agree, it is," Nora laid the plaster down on the table. "It could even have been done by youngsters back during the war. Not us. Not children. I'm thinking more of teenagers. They used to meet in there to smoke, you see. Don't know how long it went on for but eventually someone spotted them leaving and reported it to Jack Harvey who was the village bobby back then. He told their parents and it came to an abrupt halt."

"In that case it was probably teenagers that the old boy with his dog heard," reasoned Kate.

"Could have been. I don't know when the smoking sessions started but I daresay it was before we went inside ghost hunting. I think once word had it that Mavis was unlikely to come back before the war ended, it became a meeting place for lots of the older kids, especially on days when the weather was miserable."

"It was probably kids who wrote this as well then." Kate scrolled through her phone and found the picture of the, *I love Georgie* message and showed it to Nora. "Does this mean anything to you?"

"Georgie. George. Oh dear, my mind's gone blank." Nora took a piece of paper and a pen from a drawer. "Here, jot down the initials and the message on this and I'll have a think about it when you've gone."

As Kate wrote on the paper a sudden thought struck Amelia. "The other day, Ivy told us that she wasn't sure whether or not Mavis came back after the war to collect any belongings she might have left behind and I wonder if you know, Nora. I'm just thinking that perhaps she didn't come back. I mean surely she wouldn't have gone away with her children and left the key under a stone if there was anything left inside other than furniture."

"And the furniture we believe belonged to the Pengillirose Manor Estate anyway," added Dilly.

Nora nodded her head. "That's right it did and no, she didn't come back. Not herself anyway but her brother did on her behalf. Having decided not to return to Trenwalloe I assume she would have written to the estate and given notice of her tenancy. I say this because her daughter, one of the twins with whom I played, sent me a Christmas card in 1943 saying they wouldn't be coming home because she'd lost her daddy and her mummy had decided she didn't want to live in Trenwalloe anymore because they all liked living in Grandma's house more than Holly Cottage because Grandma had a bathroom."

"1943. So this would have been soon after Harold disappeared."

"That's right, it would."

"So the house must have been empty from the time they left until after the war when it was bought by Pete Richardson who installed a bathroom," mused Dilly, "Hmm, interesting, but you say her brother came back for her belongings."

"Yes, poor Mavis. I should imagine she didn't want to come back herself because the place would have held too many memories. No doubt she had to leave a few things behind though because it would have been difficult to manage lots of luggage with two children in tow. What's more after three or four years of standing empty the house would have been in a damp and sorry state and it would certainly have grieved her to see how Archie's vegetable garden was overgrown with thriving, healthy weeds. So sad, as it was once his pride and joy. He used to grow marrows, you know. Lots of them. Goodness only knows why. I mean they're not the tastiest of veg are they."

"I quite like them stuffed," admitted Amelia, "but I prefer courgettes."

"Larry made marrow curry a few years ago and believe it or not it was really nice."

Nora's nose twitched. "Not sure about that, Kate, but then I'm not really into curry. Now, marrow and ginger jam, that's a different story."

"Oh yes," agreed Amelia, "and marrow chutney. That's very tasty too."

Dilly's eyes rolled. "Can we move on from marrows and get back to Mavis's brother."

Nora chuckled. "Sorry. My fault. Anyway, I remember Mum telling me about the brother coming back and with him he had a list of things to pick up and details of where he'd find them. Some of the things he couldn't find though and that raised a few eyebrows. I don't know what they were except I heard mention of Archie's trumpet and a cuckoo clock being missing. So we can only assume the place had been burgled in their absence and probably on more than one occasion."

As she spoke Nora glanced at the kitchen clock and then shushed her guests, "Listen," she whispered.

From an adjoining room they heard the muffled sound of a cuckoo telling them it was three o'clock.

"But surely…I mean it can't be, can it?" stuttered Dilly, "It can't be the missing clock."

Nora laughed. "No, of course not, but I was so fascinated with the notion of a cuckoo clock after Mum explained to me what it was that I vowed when I was grown up I'd have one. I've had several over the years and the one in the sitting room is my third."

A look of relief crossed Dilly's face. "So I wonder what happened to the missing items and more to the point, who took them."

"I guess we'll never know and that reminds me, I knew there was something else I wanted to tell you and talking of things going missing has jogged my memory. Although in this case it's not a thing but a who. I was thinking the other night, you see, about the war and the name Maggie Jones suddenly came back to me because she went missing too. I remember her because before the war she occasionally babysat me so Mum and Dad could pop along to the pub. She was really nice and used to read me Winnie the Pooh stories."

"So when did she disappear?" Amelia was intrigued.

"Would you believe, four days after Harold was reported missing? Of course, I didn't think of her when you asked me about anyone from the village disappearing during the war simply because the remains found were those of a young male."

"Maggie Jones. Was she by any chance related to the late Patrick Jones who used to run Lower Valley Farm?" Ivy asked.

"That's right," said Nora, "Maggie was Patrick's sister. He was the younger of the two and took on the farm after their parents died. But he's been gone a fair few years now and the farm which he sold on his retirement is now a holiday complex."

"And I think I'm right in saying he never married, did he?"

"Nope. In fact he was a bit of a loner. Probably caused by his sister's disappearance."

"That's a shame because if this Patrick had no family then there's no-one for us to bombard with questions," sighed Amelia.

Dilly drummed her fingernails on the table top. "Hmm, but nevertheless this all sounds rather fascinating," she turned to Nora, "so what can you tell us about Maggie Jones?"

"Not a great deal because as I've already said back then I was only a child but all the same I was curious and used to listen to my parents discussing it even though they thought I was engrossed in reading my Enid Blyton books. Anyway, as I said she went missing four days after Harold. Rumour had it she might have gone off to join him but of course we now know that didn't happen because poor Harold never even left the village. It was all rather strange because if I remember correctly she left a note to say that she was going and not to try and find her. She gave no reason and her parents always felt something wasn't quite right. You know, perhaps she was forced to write it or it was written by someone else."

Kate frowned. "But why might they think that?"

"Well that's the strange thing. She didn't leave the note in the house, you see, but posted it through the letterbox."

"How odd," said Dilly, "Were any of her things missing?"

"Oh yes. Her suitcase had gone from the top of her wardrobe and so had most of her clothes."

"And they never heard from her again?"

"Well rumour has it they received postcards now and again to say she was fine but whether she wrote any of them I've no idea. They stopped after a while though and she never came back to the best of my knowledge. Goodness only knows what happened to her and she's no doubt been dead a while now."

"I wonder where she went and why," mused Amelia.

Nora sighed deeply. "I wish I knew, but of course with there being a war on there was a lot happening on a daily basis. Everything was topsy-turvy and Maggie Jones was soon forgotten. At least she was by most people. I daresay it preyed on the minds of her family frequently though and probably sent them all to an early grave."

Chapter Nine

Sophie Sally Sackitt arrived at Holly Cottage a week later along with her husband, Graham. With them they had the ashes of her uncle, Harold Jenkins, but they remained in the boot of the car.

Kate and Larry greeted the couple warmly and after showing them the cellar and explaining how the discovery had been made, they all sat in the newly decorated sitting room with mugs of coffee and slices of ginger cake.

For the first time that day Kate was able to relax for all morning she had worried that the meeting might be strained, but because Sophie had never known her uncle she was philosophical and showed little emotion. She was, however, willing to tell what little she knew of her uncle's disappearance which she had also relayed to the police both in Surrey and in Cornwall. Kate listened to every word intently, ready to make notes and pass on her findings to her fellow investigators at the first possible opportunity.

Sophie glanced towards the window where the roses on the arch shimmered in the golden sunlight. "I recall Mum telling me that Uncle Harold had several friends who all lived in this village. Needless to say though, they saw much less of each other after the war broke out. It was while Uncle Harold was home on leave that he disappeared. The night before he had met up with some of his friends who said that he seemed his normal self. I believe it was late summer and they all went for a walk and then sat on the beach talking about their hopes and dreams for the future. Quite sad really. Anyway, the next day his closest friend, I don't recall his name but he was on leave from the Navy, went to call for him as they had arranged to go fishing. Uncle Harold's mum, who of course was my grandmother, called up the stairs to him but there was no reply so she told whatever he was called to go up and wake him. He went up but then came straight back down. Uncle Harold wasn't in his room and his bed had not been slept in. After a bit of searching they established his rucksack and a few of his belongings were missing, and so was his bike. Two days later, a bike abandoned at the railway station was identified as belonging to Uncle Harold. Of course after that, stories of desertion were rife and that took its toll on my mother and my grandparents."

"You mother being Harold's sister, Grace Jenkins," said Kate.

"That's right. After they left Cornwall they went to live in Dorset and Mum took up nursing. She later moved to Surrey and while working in a hospital there, she met George Dowling, my dad. They married a year later and had just one child, me."

Kate looked puzzled. "Oh, Nora, an elderly lady of ninety-one who lives in the village and vaguely remembers your family from her childhood, thought your mother might have been engaged to someone in the Forces, so she must have got that wrong."

"No, no, Mum was to be engaged to a sailor but sadly the poor bloke must have died because his family were told that he was missing, presumed dead. I think that was another reason Mum was glad to leave the area. First she lost her would-be fiancé and then her only brother."

"Oh dear," sighed Kate, "that's very sad."

Larry leaned forward in his chair, a puzzled expression on his face. "Did your grandparents and your mother not see Harold then? When he returned home that evening after meeting his friends, I mean."

"Funny you should say that because it's one of the things I asked Mum when she told me about her brother. Her explanation was that rather than walk through the bar if the pub was still open, he'd use the back door and slip up to his room that way. But if the pub was closed and they were clearing up then he'd pop in and say goodnight. Mum said he was reluctant to get chatting with the locals, especially the older men who'd served in the First World War. They'd want to talk about the war, you see. A subject Uncle Harold was keen to avoid."

"Makes sense, and I know it's a big ask but do you have any idea who the other friends were that he met the night before he was found to be missing?" Larry asked.

Sophie shook her head. "How I wish I did. Mum did mention the names of some but sadly I can't remember any of them. I was only thirteen when she told me about her brother and being a typical teenager I wasn't really that interested. Having said that, some of the other friends might have been girls because I remember her saying something about local girls working in a munitions factory. Mum didn't work there though because she was in the Women's Land Army and helped out in the pub. Whether the other friends were girls, and if they were Mum's friends as well, I've no idea, but I doubt it because Uncle Harold was five years older than Mum so his friends were probably older than her too. How I wish I'd listened, especially now poor Uncle Harold has been found. One thing I do know for sure though is Mum was emphatic that her brother would never have gone away without telling her. She said they were very close and despite him being several years older than her they never kept secrets from each other."

"And the fact he's been found and appears to have been murdered backs up my mother-in-law's claim," added Graham, "Poor lady."

"It does," agreed Kate.

"To what extent were the police involved back then?" Larry asked.

"Not much. From what Mum said it never went any higher than the village bobby who just questioned my grandparents, my mum and Uncle Harold's friends. I mean, because his things were missing and his bike was found at the railway station there was no reason to think anything other than he'd gone off of his own free will for whatever reason. And I'm sure it would never have crossed the minds of anyone that he might be dead. Poor man. Mum said that because he was a bit of a flirt there was even rumour that he may have run off with one of the many girls he was besotted with but we now know that definitely wasn't the case."

"Yes, Nora said something along those lines. Maggie Jones was most likely the young lady in question and the rumour would have started because she disappeared four days after your uncle."

"Really! And was she ever found?"

"Not to my knowledge. She lived on a farm and left a note for her parents saying she was going away but not giving a reason why."

"Oh dear, her poor parents. It must have ruined their lives. I know my uncle's disappearance affected my mum and grandparents badly."

"Going back a step if I may. You said the police showed little interest in your uncle's disappearance, but how about the Army?" Larry asked, "Surely they must have been concerned."

"Oh they were certainly more concerned than the police but of course Mum and her family wouldn't have known to what extent their enquiries might have gone. They were questioned of course but heard no more. So much was kept hushed up back then."

Kate sighed deeply. "Yes, and I'm sure your poor uncle wasn't the first soldier to go AWOL."

"Nor the last," said Larry.

Sophie reached for her handbag. "I'm not sure whether you'll be interested in this but I've had a couple of copies made of an old photo." She handed a small black and white picture to Kate, "It's Uncle Harold and was taken in 1938 on his eighteenth birthday. I've given a copy to the police and if you want you're more than welcome to have this copy to keep."

Kate was overwhelmed. "What a handsome young man and yes please we'd love to keep it. Seeing his face makes him come to life," she handed the picture to Larry, "and I can assure you, Sophie, that Larry, our friends and I will do everything we can to get to the bottom of your uncle's death."

Chapter Ten

After breakfast, while Larry was out in the front garden preparing to cut the lawn, Kate reached for the notes she had made regarding the death of Harold Jenkins and placed them in her handbag along with the picture taken on his eighteenth birthday. She then walked into the village to Lavender Cottage, to relay information received from Sophie Sally Sackitt.

Kate found Dilly at home drinking coffee along with visitors, Amelia and Ivy. After Dilly had made a coffee for Kate and insisted she sample a slice of rhubarb and ginger cake in order to get her opinion of it, Kate told them of Sophie and her husband's visit and the information gleaned.

Ivy was impressed. "Well done, Kate. Now we know quite a bit more including the year he was born and we have a photo of the lovely young man, I think it's time we had a meeting with the vicar and see if he can shed any light on possible names for Harold's friends. I know he'd be willing to help as he's fascinated with John's records, pictures and so forth and I'm sure he'd be glad to put them to good use. What do you all think?"

"I think that's an excellent idea," enthused Dilly. "Without the names of Harold's friends we'll get nowhere so finding out has to be our next move. Shall we give the vicar a ring?"

"I'll do it now." Ivy pulled her mobile phone from her pocket and went out into the kitchen so that she could concentrate on the vicar's response.

"We must get Dotty, Gerry, and Robin to join us as well," said Amelia, as Ivy closed the door, "and of course Ernie will want to hear what's going on."

"Freddie and Max too," said Dilly, "oh, and Orville of course."

"My goodness, it sounds quite a houseful so where shall we meet?" Kate asked: "I'd be happy to make use of our place especially now the sitting room is decorated and we have a lovely carpet fitted. Such a treat after making do with the kitchen for so long."

"Or you can all come here," said Dilly, "It won't be the first time I'll have had a houseful."

However, Dilly and Kate's offers of their homes weren't necessary. The vicar, delighted by the notion of a fact-finding evening, said they were welcome to come to the vicarage where all John's records would be close at hand.

"Ow, smashing," said Kate. "Larry and I went past the vicarage the other day and thought it looked an interesting place. Not that we could see the house."

"It is interesting," agreed Ivy, "and the garden is a good size. So is the house for that matter. And before I forget, the vicar said he'd lay on a few refreshments but I said not to go to too much trouble as we'd all be happy to bring a plate of something as well."

Amelia chuckled. "Sounds lovely but what about drink? I know the vicar often pops in the pub for half a bitter but might he object to bottles of wine?"

Ivy returned to the chair she had vacated to make the call. "Oh, he'll be fine with that. In fact he often has a glass of wine in the evening. He says it helps him sleep."

"Even better," said Dilly, "although I think on this occasion it might be best if Ernie's homemade wine stays in your pantry, Amelia."

"Oh, don't worry, I shall tell Ernie that tonight his wine is strictly forbidden."

The vicar having stated that he would be in all day said they would be welcome at the vicarage at whatever time suited; after phone calls were made it was agreed that they should all meet from seven o'clock onwards. Dilly, Orville, Amelia and Ernie were the first to arrive and because it was a beautiful calm evening, the vicar, Peter Goodman, suggested they all sit outside on the terrace where he had pushed two picnic tables together.

"But first, please feel free to wander around the garden. It's my pride and joy and the place where I'm able to relax and be at peace with the world."

As the first four strolled off around the garden, more of the party arrived. On spotting the Greenwoods after they had concluded their tour, Dilly approached Kate. "You really must take a look around the garden, it's quite breath-taking. Our vicar certainly has green fingers."

"I'll do that because I have my gardening head on right now. Which reminds me, I've already cleared a flower bed ready for your wallflowers, Dilly. The soil seems really good so they should do well." She chuckled to herself, "I had a dear little friend to help me while I was out there. A robin was with me all the time I was digging and his song was a delight."

"A robin," said Ivy, who had overheard Kate's comment, "you know what that means, don't you?"

Kate shrugged her shoulders. "He was hungry?"

"Well yes, but actually seeing the little fella can have several other meanings as well as being hungry and two in particular relate to you and Larry. The first that springs to mind is that he popped along to see you because there's been a death at your home. Admittedly it was a long time ago and the deceased was not a family member or even a loved one. In fact you didn't even know him. Harold, I mean. But all the same it could still be a sign from above." Ivy waved her arm towards the sky: "You know, a message from the heavens to tell you the deceased is now at peace. That's if he is. On the other hand, and this is more likely, the little bird represents renewal, like a fresh start which will transform your lives. And that applies because you've just moved down here."

"Have you been on the wine already?" Orville asked Ivy.

Kate smothered a smile. "Well, thank you for that, Ivy. And there was me thinking, as I said earlier, that he'd merely paid me a visit because he was hungry."

Orville laughed. "Well if I had to put money on it I'd say your original thought was correct, Kate. Message from above and renewal. What a load of old codswallop."

Dilly wagged her finger. "There's nothing wrong with folklore, Orville, and it could be dangerous to mock it, but in this case let's split the difference and say it was a bit of both."

"Anything you say, my sweet," he blew her a kiss.

Inside the kitchen, offerings of food were arranged on the large pine table and drinks placed on the Welsh dresser. When all invited were present, the vicar suggested they partake of the refreshments first and then begin the meeting. He spoke with great enthusiasm and they hoped he might have found out something about the late Harold Jenkins.

As they walked around the kitchen table selecting items of food, Dilly looked around. "I thought Robin and Gerry would be joining us."

Dotty carefully placed a spoonful of coleslaw beside a spicy chicken drumstick. "They will but not 'til later. Gerry finishes his shift at eight and so they'll come round after he's been home to change."

"Good. The more the merrier."

When all were seated outside on the terrace the vicar asked that they put their hands together and he said Grace. As they ate, conversations around the table were little more than small talk for all were reluctant to get onto the subject of Harold Jenkins before the vicar was ready. When all the plates were empty and ready to be cleared away, the vicar asked if they were happy to remain outside or if they would rather retire to his sitting room. A show of hands was taken and the party unanimously opted to remain outdoors.

The vicar stood. "In which case, I know it's not cold, but I shall light the chiminea because its presence is a comfort." He pointed to a rotund clay object with a tall chimney. "And while I do so please help yourselves to a drink."

"Ah, so that's what it is. I did wonder." Dilly watched as the vicar lit the fire, "I've heard of them of course but never actually seen one before."

When the fire was going, plates were cleared and glasses filled, the vicar disappeared into his study and then re-joined them at the table, a file of papers beneath his arm.

"Now, I've looked through John's records but as you'd expect there's not a great deal for the war years simply because John wasn't born until 1940 so would only have been a youngster back then. For that reason I then turned to the church records and baptisms in particular. Having been told by Ivy that Harold was eighteen in 1938, my first search was for males and females baptised in the early 1920s but sadly that search was thwarted because someone must have spilled something on the relevant pages and the smudged writing is almost illegible. Nevertheless, I have been able to make out two names who would have been contemporaries of Harold Jenkins. The first is Betty Reynolds. I don't know her date of birth but she was baptised on January 21st 1921. I've also looked amongst marriages but there is no mention of her so I assume that if she married she had by then left the parish. There is also no record of her burial either but then many are cremated these days and had she married she would have changed her name. Her baptism entry shows she was the daughter of Gladys and Garth Reynolds. And here's the interesting bit, they lived in Lady Fern Lane at Willow Cottage."

Kate gasped. “Denzil’s place and our next door neighbours.”

“Precisely. Anyway, I’ve asked around and established that the Gladys and Garth Reynolds left Lady Fern Lane after the war and moved into one of the then newly built local authority houses in the village. I assume one or both of them might have worked at the Pengillirose Manor and they left in order for the whole estate to be sold, but that’s pure guess work. I do, however, know they died within a year of each other and are buried in a double grave here in the churchyard. I’ve seen it many times, you see, because it’s near to the bank where daffodils bloom in the spring and where I like to sit. Their deaths were in 1986 and 1987.”

“Hmm, so it’s possible that their daughter Betty, being a contemporary of Harold, might have been one of the young people he was with the evening before he died,” said Kate.

“That’s what I was hoping but as I’ve said, I’ve found no trace of her but I shall endeavour to continue my search.”

“And the other name?” Ivy asked, “You said there were two.”

“Yes, and the second is also female. It’s a bit smudged but reads either Arabella, Amabella or Annabella Triggs who was baptised on March 7th 1921. Her parents are listed as William and Emily Triggs and they lived at Number 3, Paradise Row in School Lane, but I believe the row of houses have long since been demolished.”

“That’s right,” agreed Ivy, “Paradise Row was demolished when I was still at school.”

“Is there anything more about the Triggs family?” Dilly asked.

“Sadly not but I do have something else that may be of interest.” He lifted out a black and white photograph of children sitting around trestle tables laden with party food. “On the back of this it says Sunday School Christmas Party 1928, but sadly there are no names to help identify any of the children." He handed the picture to Dotty, who after looking at it passed it on.

"Oh," sighed Amelia, as she glanced at the photograph before handing it to Ernie, "if only someone had written the names on the back."

"I agree," said the vicar, "but I suppose everyone who had a copy back then would have known who the children were so it wasn't necessary. Sadly, people don't always think of generations to come who'll not be in the know."

Ivy took the photograph from Dilly, keen to see if any of the children bore resemblance to current villagers. After studying the young faces she gave up and passed the picture on.

From her handbag, Kate took the photograph of Harold taken on his eighteenth birthday. None of the children resembled him but as one or two of the boys were not looking at the camera, his presence at the party could not be ruled out.

After passing the picture on, Kate addressed the vicar. "I don't suppose you've had any luck with the initials SC and AN either."

The vicar sighed deeply. "Sadly not, nor have I yet come across a George or Georgie. I must admit it's quite frustrating."

"Oh well, not to worry," sighed Larry, "I daresay the scribblings were most likely done by kids anyway."

"Or done well after the time we're looking at," conceded Amelia, "I mean, the several layers of wallpaper could have been done in a relatively short space of time by tenants of Pete Richardson."

The vicar looked puzzled. "Pete Richardson. Who might he be, Amelia?"

"He's the chap who bought the two cottages in Lady Fern Lane when the Pengillirose Estate was sold after the war. He didn't buy the manor house, or any land though. Just the two cottages."

"I see. Yes, thank you. It's nice to gather bits of history."

"What about school records," said Dilly, "Surely the primary school here has records of pupils and possibly pictures in their archives too?"

The vicar placed the Christmas party photograph in his folder as it came back to him. "That's what I'm hoping but the school is closed now until early September. I know where the headmistress lives but think it would be unacceptable to bother her during the holidays."

"Oh, I can agree with your sentiments there," said Dilly. "I well remember being stopped in the street during holidays and asked how young so-and-so is doing at sport by over enthusiastic parents."

"What's the headmistress like?" Dotty asked. "I don't think I've ever met her."

"Lovely," enthused Ivy, "charming in fact and very knowledgeable. She must be around my age so coming up for retirement I should imagine. Yes, yes, course she is. I remember her sixtieth and that's a few years ago now."

"Has she been at this school long?" Dilly asked.

"About thirty years I'd say. She came here after old Mr Bishop retired. He was rather stern and wouldn't take any old nonsense. Taught me in fact and that's more years ago than I care to remember."

Ernie frowned. "Is it really not possible to make out any names in the baptism records other than for the two girls, Vicar?"

Peter Goodman shook his head. "Sadly not and I've even looked closely with a magnifying glass."

"How frustrating, but then at least we know a bit about Harold so it doesn't really matter if his name is amongst the illegible ones."

The vicar nodded. "And Harold might not have been baptised here anyway. Because with that family being publicans it's possible they moved in from elsewhere when Harold was no longer a baby."

Ernie groaned. "True, yes. Publicans like clergymen are inclined to move around."

"But surely someone can be baptised at any age," reasoned Amelia, "Not just when a baby."

"True, true," agreed the vicar, "but had his parents wanted him baptised then it might well have been done wherever they lived before coming here. However, had he been baptised when he was older then I would have seen a record of it in later years where the pages are not damaged. As it is there is no mention of him at all and I looked as far forward as 1940 when of course he'd have long since grown up."

"What about Maggie Jones?" Dilly suddenly recalled Nora telling of her disappearance. "She had a brother too. Patrick I believe. They lived at Lower Valley Farm."

"I've seen no record of them so perhaps they too moved to the village when the children were older."

Dilly sighed. "Could be the case, I suppose."

"I've just remembered something," said Amelia, excitedly, "When John was looking into the Bray family history he used a genealogy website. Might it help if we did that?"

The vicar smiled but not in a condescending manner, "Sadly not. If we were to type in the few names and dates we have it would only help if we wanted to go backwards. As it is we need to find descendants of Harold and his friends and not their ancestors."

"Of course," Amelia looked deflated.

"I know. How about looking at the census for 1921," suggested Dilly. "Surely that would help."

"I had thought of that," acknowledged the vicar, "but census returns are done by street names and addresses so unless we know where people lived back then it'd be difficult to track anyone down. Furthermore, because the latest census available is for 1921 and the returns are always done at the end of March, anyone born after that date would not be included."

"And that's likely to be all of, or at least most of, Harold's friends," sighed Dilly.

"Exactly. Anyway, don't be too disheartened because I do have something that might interest you all." He reached amongst the papers and pulled out a small red book. "This is my grandmother's diary. At least it's one of them. As some of you will know, my grandfather was vicar here from 1944 to 1957. I looked through my grandmother's diaries to see if any of them were written during the war years and I found this one for 1944, which of course was the year they moved here." He looked at the eager eyes around the table and smiled. "Amongst other things this is what she wrote –

> *Today I was introduced to a charming young lady called Grace. She is the only daughter of the licensees of the Duck and Parrot. She spends her time working hard on the land during the day in the Women's Land Army and at night helps her parents in the public house. She struck me as a bright young thing but behind the smiles I detected a sadness in her eyes and when I asked if she had a boyfriend I found the reason why. She told me that she had a boyfriend once and they were planning to get engaged when he was next home on leave but sadly this never happened because in 1942 his parents received news that he was missing, presumed dead. She then unburdened herself by telling me of her missing brother who disappeared while home on leave in September last year. They were soulmates, she said and she missed him desperately. She then opened the clasp of a locket hanging around her neck and pointed to each of the two young men she*

had loved. One was her brother, Harold. The other her would-be fiancé, Eric Bray. My heart bleeds for her."

Dilly gasped. "Eric Bray! He was the uncle of Bert Bray from whom I bought my house, Lavender Cottage. Well, not actually from him because he had died but from his estate. Remember, Freddie, amongst the Bray's things left in the old sideboard we found a telegram from the War Office notifying Eric's parents that he was missing, presumed dead. It was dated 1942 so it has to be him."

"I remember it well. And wasn't there a photo of him in one of the old albums. If I remember correctly he was in uniform."

"You're right and he was in uniform. I'll look out the albums later when I get home. With any luck some of the old snaps might be of Eric's contemporaries and now we know what Harold looks like, perhaps some will be of him."

Chapter Eleven

Inside the Duck and Parrot, Gerry and Robin propped up the bar, pints in hand and each with an open packet of crisps on the counter.

"I thought you two'd be at the vicarage tonight," said Landlord, Robert Stevens, as he placed clean wine glasses on a shelf above the till. "Orville was in at lunchtime and he said you were all having a meeting there tonight to discuss the latest on young Harold Jenkins."

"We'll be going there shortly." Gerry pushed his mobile phone in the pocket of his jacket and dropped it onto the floor by his bar stool, "but I only finished work at eight and after popping home to change I asked Rob if he fancied a beer before we went to join the others and as you can gather he said yes."

"Fair enough." Seeing someone enter the bar, Robert went to serve them.

Gerry, having not divulged the real reason for their proposed late entrance at the gathering, smothered a smile. For the two young men had already discussed an evening at the vicarage and thought it might not be to their liking. They imagined very few home comforts and having to sit on hard dining chairs around a table in a sparsely furnished room with a single pendula light dangling from a high ceiling while they ate cucumber sandwiches and listened to Bach.

"Fancy another?" Gerry drained his glass and placed it on the bar.

"Okay. Go on then but we mustn't be too late as I should imagine that girlfriend of yours has quite a temper. She's not daft and knows you were due to finish work at eight."

"Oh, don't worry about Dotty. Her bark's far worse than her bite. Besides, she's got all her mates so she won't miss us and probably wouldn't notice if we didn't turn up at all."

"If you're thinking of giving it a miss altogether I'd think again. And as for Dotty not noticing our absence I think you under estimate her because she strikes me as pretty switched on."

"Yeah, I suppose she is but don't worry, we'll go but in our own sweet time." To emphasise the point Gerry ordered two more pints.

As they finished their fourth pints and contemplated a fifth, Robert nodded towards the clock at the end of the bar. "As much as it goes against the grain to turn away trade I really think you two had better make a move."

Gerry glanced at the clock and gasped. "Oh, for Pete's sake. Look it's nearly half past nine. Where did the last hour go? Come on, Rob, let's go or we'll both be in the doghouse." His bravado gone he stepped down from the barstool and picked up his jacket. Robin did likewise.

There was very little light left and stars were beginning to emerge in the darkening sky as they walked through the vicarage gates and strolled along the short, tree lined driveway. On reaching the large detached house they saw it was in total darkness.

"Looks like there's no-one here," whispered Robin, "No lights in any of the rooms. Perhaps they've all gone home already."

"Well, we'll knock and see. Then we can apologise and we'll tell the vicar I had to work late. He won't query it."

Robin looked aghast. "You can't tell lies to a vicar, Gerry. It just wouldn't be right."

"No, I suppose not. Oh well, let's play it by ear."

Gerry rapped the old brass knocker and stepped back as they heard its sound reverberate in the hallway. For a minute or two nothing happened. They were about to leave when a lamp above the doorway lit up the gravel path and the door slowly creaked opened. "Oh, it's you two," said Ivy, her cheeks clearly glowing in the lamplight. "Come on in." She closed the door behind them. "Where on earth have you been? Dotty's tried to ring you at least three times."

"She has?" Gerry bit his bottom lip. He remembered his phone was on silent and he'd heard it vibrating from his jacket pocket on the floor of the pub, but had chosen to ignore it.

"I can hear music," hissed Robin, as they followed Ivy along the hallway and into the kitchen. She turned to them and pointed to the large pine table, "There are a few bits of food left in these containers if you're hungry. Meanwhile, we're all out here."

She led them through the back door and into the gardens. The mouths of both young men gaped open. Around the chiminea sat the small gathering, glasses in hands as music rang from a CD player and Dotty, an avid dancer, jived with Orville as Bill Haley and his Comets 'rocked around the clock'. On the tables and around the terrace hung jars containing flickering candles. Voices were raised: not in aggression but in a happy way along with peals of laughter. On spotting the new arrivals, the vicar stood up to greet them and after shaking their hands, he picked up a bottle of wine. "Will you join us for a drink, lads?"

Just before eleven, the vicar's guests agreed it was time to leave. As they passed between the gateposts and stepped out onto the pavement, discussing the evening's outcome, Ivy glanced up at the church tower. "You'll probably think me mad, bonkers even, or say I've had one too many glasses of wine, but I feel, well, how shall I put it, spiritual right now. Yes, spiritual. And please don't laugh but I wonder, do you think it might be a good idea if I were to sit all alone in the cellar to see if I feel any sort of presence? Or sense anything that might give us a clue as to who took poor Harold's life? I don't mean now, of course, but perhaps another day or even night. Well, not the middle of the night, more early evening."

Dilly paused and looked at Ivy's earnest face. "Are you serious?"

"Absolutely."

"Well rather you than me."

"I think it's an excellent idea," enthused Dotty, "and if we're all in the house too, Ivy will have plenty of backup if she gets scared and shouts for help."

"I won't be scared. As you know I'm fascinated by spiritualism and what have you and I have no fear of the afterlife. I certainly don't think anyone or anything would harm me."

"I'm game," said Ernie, "but what say you, Kate, Larry? After all it's your cellar, in your place so it can't be done without your approval."

"I'm, well, rather overwhelmed by the idea," Kate admitted, "but it could be fun if nothing else."

Larry took his wife's arm. "And I feel the same."

"Good, thank you everyone. Meanwhile, well let's sleep on it tonight and perhaps arrange something in the morning."

All agreed and then made their way to their respective homes.

On arriving back at Lavender Cottage, Dilly, feeling wide awake and wanting to clear her head of muddled thoughts, took Ben, the black Labrador who had belonged to John Martin, the deceased local historian, for a stroll along the beach. The evening was still and the sea calm; stars twinkled in the black velvet sky and a beam of moonlight flickered on the gently falling waves. Confident the tide was ebbing she walked across the compressed, wet sand, Ben loyally by her side. As they reached boulders she sat down and threw Ben's ball towards the slipway where small boats including inflatables, dinghies, kayaks and canoes were moored. The dog, energetic despite his age, tore after it and returned, panting, tail wagging, for more.

Dilly sighed. "If only your master was still here, Ben. I'm sure he'd have found out much more than we have but it's not for the want of trying. There must be something we're missing. Something glaringly obvious but for the life of me I can't think what it might be." As the ball left her fingers and flew once again towards the slipway, she looked to the heavens. "Please help us, John. Help us get justice for young Harold. The poor lad deserves it." Feeling chilly as a sudden breeze ruffled her hair, she called Ben to her side whereupon they returned to Lavender Cottage and locked out the night.

Chapter Twelve

The following morning, as Kate washed the breakfast dishes thinking about the meeting at the vicarage and Ivy's suggestion of spending time in the cellar, it suddenly occurred to her that it might also be worthwhile paying Elsie Mitchell a visit in the care home where she lived. For although Elsie would have been very young when the Jenkins family ran the pub, and Kate wasn't even sure that she had lived in the village prior to marrying, she might have picked up some useful information during the sixty or so years she had lived at Holly Cottage. Eager to relay her thoughts she rang Dilly to see if she might be of the same opinion; to her delight Dilly agreed a visit could well be productive.

"Wonderful. Now, I know it's the Pendilly Cove Care Home that she's in but I've no idea where it is, so can you help me there?"

"No, I'm afraid not, but Ivy will know. Leave it with me for a minute, Kate. I'll give her a ring and then get back to you. At the same time I'll also ask if she's had any more thoughts about her lonely vigil."

Ivy not only knew where the care home was but was acquainted with Jenny and Terry Carne, the married couple who ran it. To help out she said she'd give the home a ring to make sure a visit would be okay as she didn't want them to have a wasted trip should Elsie be unwell or otherwise engaged.

Ten minutes later, Ivy rang back to say that Elsie was in very good health and would be delighted to receive visitors.

She also said that she'd be happy to sit in the cellar whenever it was convenient for Kate and Larry.

"Excellent," said Kate, as Dilly relayed the news. "I think we should strike while the iron's hot and probably have everyone here tonight. Then while Ivy does her meditating or whatever, the rest of us can chew over what we learned at the vicarage last night as well as anything Elsie might have to say."

"Lovely, yes. I'll ring around then and see if everyone else agrees."

"Before you do, what about the care home visit? Shall I go on my own or would you like to go with me?"

"I'd love to meet the lady but perhaps it might be best if you went on your own as we don't want to overwhelm her."

"True, but on the other hand, if Elsie is able to pass on any useful bits of information, having two of us there might mean nothing gets missed."

"That's a good point, Kate. So when are you thinking of going?"

"I think it's a bit late to go this morning now so how about this afternoon?"

"Yes, fine by me."

"Lovely, I'll pick you up at half two."

"I'll be ready and waiting."

"By the way, did you find the photograph album you mentioned last night, the one with a picture of Eric thingy, Grace Jenkins' boyfriend in it?"

"Eric Bray. Yes, I did but sadly none of the other pictures shed any light on our efforts. They're mostly of family but then I suppose people didn't take pictures as frequently in the early forties. In fact many wouldn't even have owned a camera."

"Bit different today with everyone taking everything on mobile phones."

"Absolutely."

"Anyway, not to worry at least we know a tiny bit about Grace when she was young and we have a picture of Harold. What's more, I'm sure we'll get there in the end."

Dilly chuckled. "I admire your optimism, Kate. I really do."

Pendilly Cove Care Home was situated one and a half miles away from the village as the crow flies and three miles by road. Once a hotel, the three storey, granite built building had twelve residential rooms, a kitchen, a dining room, a large residents' lounge, numerous bathrooms and a reception room-cum-office. Kate parked in the car park beneath a horse chestnut tree and together she and Dilly made their way towards the double front doors.

"Wow, this is some impressive looking place." Dilly paused to watch clouds gliding over the tall chimney pots. "It must cost an arm and a leg to live here."

Inside the vestibule they were greeted by Jenny Carne who after asking them to sign the visitor's book, took them to the second floor where Elsie had a room. Having been primed up about the impending visit, Elsie had insisted on wearing her best floral print dress to greet her callers. Jenny tapped on the door and opened it gently. "Your visitors are here, Elsie." She then stepped aside to allow Kate and Dilly to enter the room where they found the elderly lady sitting in a wingback armchair beside a window with extensive views out over the sea. Jenny left as Elsie held out her hands to greet her callers. "How lovely to meet you both. I hope you don't mind me being up here. It's just that I prefer to be on my own most of the time as it gets a little noisy in the residents' lounge if the television is on and some residents whose hearing is impaired are inclined to speak in raised voices." She beckoned to them to take a seat. "I'm so lucky. You see my hearing is much like it was when I was young.

It must be awful struggling to hear, so the poor souls have my sympathy."

"I agree," said Dilly. "It must be dreadful to lose one's sight too. But sadly we're all guilty of taking our senses for granted."

"Oh, we are. Now please sit down. Knowing you were coming to see me, Jenny has kindly brought in an extra chair." As they sat Elsie looked at each visitor in turn. "Now which of you is Mrs Greenwood who along with your husband bought my dear old house?"

Kate raised her hand. "Me, and please call me Kate."

"I'd be delighted to and you must call me Elsie. So how are you and your husband getting along in the house? You've settled in by now no doubt."

"Yes, we have and I'm sure you'll be pleased to know we both love the place very much."

"Oh, I'm so delighted. It's a dear house and such a lovely peaceful location." She turned to Dilly. "And so who might you be, my dear?"

"I'm Dilys. Dilys Granger but everyone calls me Dilly. I live at Lavender Cottage in Trenwalloe Sands."

Elsie's eyes shone. "In Bertie Bray's old place?"

"Yes, that's right. Did you know him?"

"Oh yes. A lovely man and so were his parents." She leaned back in her chair. "Well Bertie's not been gone that long so you'll both be relatively new to Trenwalloe."

"We are," said Kate, "which means we've a lot to learn about the place and of course its people."

"And a lovely place it is and the people are nice too." Elsie rested her hands on her lap. "So how are things in the village? Jenny tries to keep me up to date but she doesn't live there now because she and Terry live here. The house too, I often wonder how it's doing. We were there a long time, you know. 1962 it was when Tom and me moved in and I was just a young girl then of twenty-three. Of course we didn't own the place back then. We rented it off Pete

Richardson who bought it when the old manor house, its land, and what have you were sold off after the war. But he was a good landlord, was Pete, and after we'd been there ten years he asked if we'd like to buy it from him. We jumped at the chance and never once regretted it. Anyway, never mind about me prattling on." She took Kate's hand, "tell me what you've done so far and what else you plan to do."

Using her phone, Kate showed Elsie pictures of the white marble effect floor tiles in the kitchen and the newly fitted units. She then explained how they had knocked the two living rooms into one and that a shower had been fitted in the bathroom. However, the discovery of Harold Jenkins and the opening up of the cellar she did not mention, for Jenny Carne, prior to their visit, had asked them to avoid the subject. The reason being, she believed that if Elsie found out there had been a body lying beneath the floors throughout her long residency she would be very much distressed.

Elsie glanced towards the window where a beam of sunlight shone across the pillows onto her single bed. "And the roses, are they in flower on the old metal arch yet?"

"Yes, they are and the scent from the blooms is glorious. I wish I'd thought then I could have brought a bunch of them for you."

"Oh, the scent, yes I remember it well. Tom put that arch up and I planted the roses. It were a few years ago, mind you, and as you'll have seen the arch isn't quite as pronounced as it once was but we still loved it."

Kate took Elsie's hand. "We love it too and I promise it'll stay for as long as we live at Holly Cottage."

As Kate released her hand, Elsie spotted a small silver crucifix hanging around Kate's neck. "That reminds me," she chuckled, pointing to the necklace, "Have you painted over the outline of a cross above the fireplace in the kitchen?"

Kate was taken aback by the question. "Yes, we have. The wall is snow-white now and we have our calendar hanging there."

Elsie nodded. "That'll probably be on the nail my Tom put in. You see, when we first moved to Holly Cottage we noticed the outline of the cross but thought nothing of it. We'd heard about Archie and Mavis Penrose, the manor house's former employees and tenants, from folks in the village, you see, and because they said that Mavis was very religious we assumed she'd had a crucifix hanging there. So Tom pulled out the small nail that was there, filled the small hole, and then as you've done we painted over it. But, it kept coming back. Time and time again we painted over it but it wouldn't stay hidden. That's why in the end Tom banged in another nail and we hung a picture there."

"Really! Good heavens I'd no idea it'd been there that long. We assumed the cross had been yours, you see, and the outline was left after you took it down and moved here."

"No, no, it didn't belong to either me or Tom. We were churchgoers but never had a crucifix on the wall."

"In which case I must check when I get home but I'm sure it'll not be there now."

"Well, I'd be interested to know. We were there for sixty years and so was the outline of the cross. We thought it was rather spooky."

"How strange," Kate laughed nervously realising that if the image of the cross was from a crucifix that had belonged to Mavis and not Elsie as they had assumed, then it was highly likely that the crucifix in question was the very one found along with the remains of Harold Jenkins. It wouldn't be possible to check if there was a match with the outline when she went home because although the pocket watch had been given to Sophie Sackitt, the old rug and the cross were still with the police.

Dilly, sensing Kate's thoughts was unsure how to follow up Elsie's comment but to her relief and the relief of Kate no further word was necessary. They were able to change the subject when a staff member arrived with three teas and a plate of biscuits. Over their refreshments the ladies then chatted about flowers, houses and village life and Kate told of her plans to widen the stream at the bottom of their back garden to create a small pond.

"Funny you should think about doing that because we always said it'd be nice to create a pond. We liked the idea because being part of the stream meant we wouldn't get stagnant water, but we just never got round to it." She chuckled, "can't come up with a good excuse though. I mean, we were there for sixty years so I can hardly say we didn't have the time."

"In that case so it doesn't end up the same with us, I'll make sure we start it before the end of summer."

"Is the vicar still in the village?" Elsie suddenly asked, "Peter Goodman, I mean."

"Yes, he is," said Kate. "In fact we had a small gathering at the vicarage only last night. Lovely man."

"Yes, he's a good man and lives up to his name," Elsie chuckled at her pun. "He likes to see people enjoying themselves as long as they behave, of course. I wonder, does he still have a pantry full of wine?"

"I don't know about full but he did offer us a glass or two last night." Kate was confused by the question.

"Yes, at a PCC meeting years ago he let slip he likes a glass of wine in the evenings. Said it helps him sleep and stimulates the mind when contemplating subjects for his sermons. Of course word got out, spread like wildfire, and ever since he's been given bottles of wine as presents. You know, at Christmas, as a thank you for christenings, weddings, and even funerals. For that reason he always welcomed the opportunity to have people round to the vicarage to help him drink it."

"Like us last night," said Dilly. "That explains the Welsh dresser groaning with bottles."

Kate frowned. "What's a PCC?"

"Stands for parochial church council. Tom and I were both on the Council but I stepped down after he died."

After an hour, Kate and Dilly stood to take their leave. For although the visit to the care home had not revealed any useful information as regards the death of Harold Jenkins, it was obvious Elsie enjoyed their company, which prompted them to say they would call again very soon.

Back at Holly Cottage, as Kate was telling Larry about her visit, she suddenly remembered Elsie's comments about the outline of a crucifix. Chuckling to herself she walked over to the fireplace and took down the calendar. Her face dropped. There, just as Elsie had said was the faded outline of the cross. Convinced the coat of paint must have been put on far too thinly, she went over the area again with a coat so thick that she feared the paint might run. Once done she tidied the newly extended sitting room ready for the evening's guests and then made a pasta bake for dinner. Because they had had a buffet the previous evening at the vicarage, it was agreed that everyone eat before descending on Holly Cottage to see the outcome of Ivy's spiritualistic skills. However, Kate thought it highly likely that a few bottles of wine would arrive along with the guests.

At ten minutes past eight, Dotty, Robin and Gerry, the last to arrive, took their seats in Kate and Larry's newly extended sitting room. As Larry poured them drinks, Kate asked: "Well, we're all here now, so what's next?"

Ivy drank the last of her wine, placed the empty glass on the table, stood and picked up the large bag she had nestled by her feet. "Time for me to get going, I suppose."

"Are you really sure you want to go ahead with this, Ivy?" Dilly thought the notion of sitting in any cold, damp cellar was bad enough but why anyone would even consider doing so in one where human remains had lain for eighty years was hard to comprehend.

"I'm not in the least bit worried," said Ivy, "in fact I'm quite looking forward to it."

"Come on then. Let's go." Kate escorted Ivy into the kitchen and one or two others followed. From inside the cupboard Kate flicked on the light switch, opened the trapdoor and Ivy descended the steep steps. At the bottom she took from her bag seven mauve candles which she placed around the room and in particular the spot where Harold had lain for eighty years. When the candles were lit, the sweet scent of lavender filled the area part masking the musty smell. From her bag Ivy then took a cushion and placed it on the second step up. Peering up at five faces watching her through the open trapdoor, she said: "you can leave me now but please turn out the light and close the door."

As the light went out, Ivy lowered herself onto the cushion and leaned against the wall. From the kitchen she heard voices and then all was quiet. With hands clasped tightly on her lap, she breathed in the lavender's perfume, closed her eyes and whispered Harold's name. For ten long minutes all was silent and then she heard a faint rustle. Was it the sound of shuffling feet or was it a mouse? She opened her eyes and watched for movement. All was still save the flickering flames of the candles. As she relaxed her shoulders, she heard a faint, distant sob. Abruptly it stopped and Ivy heard mumblings of the Lord's Prayer. Her eyes flashed. She was on edge. Who was sobbing? Was it Harold or was her imagination playing tricks? Feeling chilled she pulled her thick cardigan tightly across her chest and watched as the tips of her fingers turned white with the cold. In the corner where Harold had been found, the two candles flickered brightly and then went out. Ivy gasped. There were no draughts in the cellar. She heard shuffling again and surely she could smell a cigarette burning. Was it in her head? She jumped as something touched her shoulder. Not wanting to hear more she dashed up the steps and forcibly pushed open the trapdoor. From the sitting room she heard footsteps coming towards her. Glad to see her friends she stepped out onto the understairs cupboard floor. Her face was white. Without speaking, Dilly and Amelia each took one of Ivy's arms and escorted her back into the sitting room. Kate switched on the cellar light, descended the steps, blew out the remaining candles and picked up the cushion. She shrugged her shoulders. The cellar seemed and felt as normal. Convinced that whatever had frightened Ivy was no longer there, she left the cellar, closed the trapdoor and turned out the light.

Inside the sitting room the colour was slowly returning to Ivy's face as she recounted her unnerving experience. However, after concluding her - at the time - realistic account she smiled broadly realising just how silly it sounded.

"I suppose I just have an over active imagination," she confessed, "but it seemed so real at the time."

Orville patted her hand in an assuring manner. "Well, let's analyse it, shall we? Starting with the two candles going out. I mean, candles do go out for no apparent reason, don't they, so there's nothing to be spooked by in that. What's more, when they went out they might have left behind a residue of smoke which you mistook for a cigarette."

Ivy nodded. "Yes, I'll grant you that."

"And the cold down there. Well, it is cold," said Larry. "I mean, it never gets the sun and the damp makes it feel cold too. I thought that when I cleared it out and did the electrics."

"Yes, it is cold down there," agreed Kate, "What's more, the shuffling sound you heard, Ivy, could well have been someone in here moving a chair. After all the cellar is underneath this room."

"But what about the sobbing and mumblings of the Lord's Prayer?" asked Amelia. "That's what spooked me."

Robin shrugged his shoulders. "I should imagine as Ivy said it's the results of an over active imagination."

Ivy nodded her agreement but said nothing.

"I was just thinking," said Dotty, "about poor Harold being shut up down there and I wonder why someone went to the trouble of wrapping him in a rug and placing a cross with him. I mean, I'm not in the habit of murdering people but if I did then I'm sure I wouldn't have done that."

"Yes, I see where you're coming from," agreed Dilly. "It's almost as though the killer gave Harold a Christian burial. As you say, Dotty, it doesn't make sense."

Gerry drained his glass and opened another can of lager. "I don't know. The criminal mind works differently to you and I, so it's even possible that it was done in mockery. Perhaps Harold was a believer and his killer an atheist. Something like that."

"I was thinking along the same lines," said Robin, "the trouble is with it having happened so long ago there's just nothing to go on. We don't even know who his friends were let alone his enemies, if he had any."

"No, but one thing I think we can be pretty sure of is that whoever bumped Harold off and sealed him in a tomb has to be male and a fit, strong, healthy one at that," said Larry.

"Why do you say that with such emphasis?" Amelia asked.

"Because whoever the killer was would have lugged a dead weight down the cellar steps, wrapped him in the rug and positioned him in the corner. Then he'd have bricked up the cellar's entrance. Women didn't do building work back then. They were housewives. They wouldn't have access to building materials and even if they did they certainly wouldn't know how to use them."

Kate glared at her husband in disbelief. "You male chauvinist pig. Let me remind you that during the war women had no choice but to do the work of men. They worked on the land, made weapons and even built a bridge in London across the Thames."

"While I agree wholeheartedly," Dilly, amused by Kate's indignant face, smothered a smile, "and I do know how to mix cement, Larry's controversial comment does have a point. Where did the bricks come from and likewise the cement and sand? The killer would have needed a bucket too in which to mix it up. All are not things that every household has to hand. Well, most have a bucket but not sand and cement."

"Good point," said Dotty, "which more or less proves the murder was premeditated then. I should imagine the killer lured Harold here under false pretences, bumped him off in the kitchen with a blow to his head, dragged him into the cellar, wrapped him in the rug and then sealed it up having brought the building stuff along with him earlier and hidden it in the garden or something like that."

Robin laughed, "Yes, but that's nothing more than hypotheses, Dotty. I could just as easily say it was a lover's tiff and he hit his head on the corner of a table when his lady love gave him a push. There's nothing even to indicate he died in this house or for how long he'd been dead when he was placed in the cellar. We can come up with all sorts of theories but with no clues, no evidence, no witnesses and no suspects, it's unlikely this case will ever be solved. Which is a real shame because when you, Dotty, first mentioned I could help solve this case I was thrilled to bits, but now I see it as a non-starter."

Chapter Thirteen

Jamie Greenwood and his best friend Mike arrived at Holly Cottage the following day. Kate had agreed with her daughter-in-law, Jamie's mother, beforehand not to mention the remains of Harold Jenkins having been found in their cellar in case it caused Jamie's friend, Mike, to have nightmares. This was something they knew he had been badly afflicted with when much younger and although they understood from Mike's parents that he no longer suffered from claustrophobia and had outgrown his fear of the dark, they didn't want to risk anything that might trigger his old anxieties.

However, things didn't turn out quite as planned for no sooner had the boys dropped their suitcases in the hallway after their journey from the railway station in St Austell where Larry had met them, than Jamie asked, "So where's this cellar you found the dead bloke in?"

Kate was taken aback. "How did you know about that?"

"I heard Mum and Dad talking about it. They were in the garden at the time and I was in my bedroom: the window was open so they didn't know I could hear. Anyway, they said something about how they hoped if we found out about the dead bloke that it wouldn't give Mike nightmares. They seem to have forgotten he's grown up now and doesn't have nightmares anymore. That's right, mate, isn't it?"

"Yep, haven't had one for yonks."

Jamie nodded. "Exactly, and I told Mum and Dad I'd heard what they said and I insisted you were okay now but they still went ahead and had a chat with your parents. I'm sorry about that, mate."

“Ah, not to worry. I suppose they had my best interests at heart.”

“Yes, I’m sure they did,” smiled Kate.

“Without doubt,” Larry agreed, “and it’s a relief to hear that you’re okay now, Mike.”

“Thanks, so can we see the cellar now, Mr Greenwood?”

“Of course, but please, call me Larry. Mr Greenwood makes me sound like a stuffy old schoolmaster.”

Kate giggled. “And please call me Kate.”

“That’s settled that then, so come on boys and follow me.” Larry led the boys into the kitchen, opened the door to the understairs cupboard and pointed to the floor. “Well, there it is, so help yourselves.”

Jamie eagerly unbolted the trapdoor and looked into the darkness. “You won’t shut us in there, will you?”

“Of course not.” Larry flicked a switch, flooding the cellar with a bright light and even though the candles had been removed, he detected a slight scent of lavender drifted up through the square opening. Not wanting to explain the origin of the fragrance, Larry hoped neither boy would notice.

Jamie, followed by Mike, slowly crept down the steep steps touching the wall as he went. On reaching the bottom, he cast his eyes around the empty space, “Cool, and spooky too.”

“Yuck. Creepy more like.” Mike shuddered. “In fact too creepy for me. Perhaps I am still claustrophobic and afraid of the dark after all.” He turned on his heels, “I’m going back up.”

“But it’s not dark you wuss. The light’s on.” Jamie then pointed to an object lying on the floor alongside the steps. “What’s that rusty old thing, Granddad?”

“A vice,” said Larry. “Must have belonged to Archie Penrose, who used to be the maintenance man at the old manor. It weighs a ton and that’s why it’s still there. There were other tools as well but I’ve cleaned them up and they're in my tool box now. I'm not sure what to do with the vice though. I've no use for it, but it seems a shame to chuck it out."

Back in the kitchen, Kate ran her fingers across the thick coat of paint she had plastered over the imprint of the crucifix above the fireplace. It was dry, hadn't run and there was no trace of the recurring image of the cross. Pleased with her effort, she placed the calendar back on the nail and made a mental note to tell Elsie of her achievement when next they visited her at the care home.

While the boys were unpacking their belongings in their allocated rooms at Holly Cottage, Peter Goodman, the vicar, was taking a stroll around the village breathing in the fresh air, listening to birdsong and appreciating the beauties of nature. As he neared the end of Smuggler's Lane he saw Claudia Howard, headmistress of the village school approaching from the opposite direction.

He bowed his head as they met. "Good afternoon, Ms Howard."

"Good afternoon, Vicar. Lovely day for a walk."

"Oh yes. We're very lucky to live in such a beautiful part of the world."

"We are indeed." She raised the small basket in her hand: "and this year there is an abundance of lovely fat sloes. I've been picking them to make sloe gin. My favourite tipple come Christmas."

"Well done. It's good to know they'll not go to waste although I'm sure many of God's creatures enjoy them too."

"They do but there are plenty for us all." The headmistress took a step closer to the vicar. "Please don't think I'm speaking out of turn but I've heard on the grapevine that you and several others are trying to establish the identity of any young people who might have been contemporaries of poor Harold Jenkins. Is that correct?"

"Indeed it is. The several others you refer to are a dedicated group of enthusiasts who want justice for the poor lad. And that includes the current owners of Holly Cottage who had the misfortune to discover the body of the deceased."

"Hmm, not a pleasant find by any stretch of the imagination."

"No, but they seem sanguine about the situation and are taking it in their stride."

"Have you had any luck? Finding contemporaries of Harold Jenkins, that is."

"Not really. The only names I've found from the early nineteen-twenties are Betty Reynolds, and Arabella, Amabella or Annabella Triggs, whose name was difficult to read, and we've no idea what happened to either of them. Betty's parents stayed in the village until they died in the late nineteen-eighties and both are buried in the churchyard. But there's no record of Arabella, Amabella or Annabella or her parents after her baptism."

"Reynolds. Triggs. No, can't say that I've ever come across either of those names. How about Patrick Jones who used to run Lower Valley Farm? He'd be the right sort of age surely. I remember him, you see, because he sold the farm after he retired and that was in the early nineties shortly after I arrived at the school. Nice chap but very quiet."

"Patrick Jones. Yes, Dilly mentioned that name at our meeting. He had a sister too. Maggie, I think Dilly said. We drew a blank though because there is no record of their baptisms."

Claudia smiled. "Maybe their family were of a different faith or dare I suggest it, atheists."

"Very good point."

"Perhaps I can help. School records go way back beyond the nineteen-twenties. I mean, even if Maggie and Patrick's parents didn't attend church, any children they had would have attended the school and the same goes for all other families. Unless they were educated at home of course but that's quite rare now and would have been even more so backalong."

"We had thought of that but didn't want to bother you during the school holiday. I know how hard you work."

"Oh, goodness me I'd be only too happy to help, Peter. As you know I live alone so my time is my own. Furthermore, to be honest, I too would like to know just what did happen to the unfortunate young man."

Chapter Fourteen

On Friday morning, Orville watched with interest from the sitting room window of his home on the Buttercup Field Estate as a removal van pulled up outside the semi-detached bungalow opposite. He knew the elderly couple who lived there had sold and were moving up-country to be nearer their son and his family, however, he knew nothing of their successors and was curious to see who they might be. Knowing it would be a few hours until they arrived he turned his attention to selecting songs for the Male Voice Choir's next performance.

The removal van and his old neighbours left shortly before lunchtime and an hour later the new people arrived but it wasn't possible to work out who amongst the band of helpers his new neighbours might be. Only one thing he did feel sure about was that because the helpers were all young and likely to be friends of the new arrivals then surely they would be young also. His surmise proved correct for after the removal van drove away and the helpers also left, just two cars remained on the driveway. Orville watched with interest as a young couple emerged from the front door and sat down side by side on the sunny doorstep with mugs in their hands. Feeling a sudden urge to greet the newcomers, Orville crossed the road and welcomed them to Trenwalloe Sands.

In the late afternoon, as they drove back from a trip to the garden centre, Kate asked Dilly and Amelia if they'd like to call in and see Elsie as they would be passing quite near to the care home. The ladies agreed, especially Amelia who had yet to be introduced to the previous owner of Holly Cottage. Having the approval of her friends, Kate turned off the main road and into a lane. As she pulled into the care home's car park, she was surprised to see a large number of vehicles parked outside and balloons fluttering in the breeze around the entrance. When they stepped into the vestibule the reason became apparent. One of the residents was celebrating her one hundredth birthday and because there was a party atmosphere, Elsie was in the residents' lounge wearing her best dress. When she saw the ladies enter the room, her face lit up.

"How lovely to see you all again," she clasped their hands in turn, "and you've chosen the right day too because it's Mabel's one hundredth birthday. Isn't that wonderful! She's the one wearing the yellow daisy dress."

"One hundred." Kate pulled up a chair and sat down beside Elsie. "It certainly is wonderful and she looks amazing for her age." She took Amelia's arm, "and before we forget, this lady is Dilly's next door neighbour, Amelia Trewella."

Elsie shook her hands warmly. "I'm very pleased to meet you, and I love your name, Amelia. It's what I called my favourite doll many years ago."

"Thank you. I like my name as well but I know lots of people are unhappy with their parents' choice." Amelia pulled up a chair on the other side of Elsie. Dilly opted for a stool by Elsie's feet. "So, what's the secret of Mabel's longevity?" Dilly was intrigued.

"I've no idea. Perhaps it's a healthy lifestyle or maybe it's the glass of sherry she has each evening."

Kate was equally intrigued. "Any idea where she lived before she came here?"

"I believe it was in Mevagissey and she was married to a fisherman. Yes, of course she was because I remember her telling me now that his name was Tom, Tom Bennett. Same as my dear husband except of course my Tom wasn't Tom

Bennett he was Tom Mitchell and he wasn't a fisherman he was a fireman. I'm rambling, aren't I?"

"No," said Dilly, "no you're not. It's good for you to reminisce."

Elsie glanced in Mabel's direction. "I've not really spoken to her much but then as you know I'm inclined to stay in my room. I did sit next to her once for dinner though and we had a bit of a chat and a good laugh too. She can be very funny and is really popular here as you can see by the turn out today."

As she spoke two of the carers wheeled in a large cake on a trolley. Amongst the sugar paste roses, one hundred candles flickered in the draught from an open window. After the residents, carers and visitors sang happy birthday, Mabel surprised one and all by blowing out every candle in one puff.

"Hey, well done, darlin'," said an elderly man sitting by her side, "as you know it took me two attempts to blow out mine."

Mabel slapped his thigh in a good-natured manner. "Thank you, sweetheart. I've always had a good pair of lungs. I put it down to swimming every day until I reached my eightieth."

Elsie turned to her guests. "The young man who just spoke is Mabel's boyfriend. He's a retired gardener, is as fit as a fiddle and used to live in Truro. A couple of years ago the dear man celebrated his one hundredth birthday but of course I wasn't here back then."

Dilly gasped. "So he's one hundred and two. But that's amazing."

"We put it down to the Cornish air," said Elsie, with pride. "Nothing quite like it."

Kate was rendered speechless by the notion of having a one hundred and two year old boyfriend.

Shortly after Dilly arrived back at Lavender Cottage, Orville called round with a bunch of sweet peas picked from his own garden. "I know you like the scent of these so thought

I'd pop round with some." His eyes twinkled. "Got some news as well."

"Really! Do tell."

As Orville took a seat in the living room, Dilly arranged the flowers in a jug.

"The folks in a bungalow across the road from me moved out this morning and a young couple have moved in. They're from Ipswich and I should imagine they're in their early thirties. They're called Libby and Luke and both work for the NHS so I assume they've done a transfer. You'll like them, they were really friendly and said they're keen to get into surfing. I told them they were in the right place and that the pub's licensees have a son called Dylan who is a surfing instructor and lifeguard. They were thrilled to bits and said they'd pop along to the pub as soon as they got straight. But the interesting thing is their name, although I suppose it's quite common really, because it's Reynolds."

"Reynolds! Hmm, I can see where you're coming from. You're wondering if they might be related to Betty who we don't seem able to trace."

"That's exactly what I'm thinking, although as I said it's a common enough name but there is a chance that Luke might be returning to his roots. Not Libby of course because she'll have had a different name before she married Luke."

Dilly placed the jug of flowers in the middle of the table. "And you reckon they're in their early thirties?"

"Yes. Mid-thirties possibly but certainly no older than that."

"So there's a slim chance, and I emphasise slim, that he, this Luke chappie, could be, say, Betty's grandson or even her great grandson." She sat down and then shook her head, "No, but he can't, can he? Because had Betty married and had children, and then those children had had children, their name would not be Reynolds, would it? Betty's name would be whatever the bloke she married was called."

"Oh, fiddlesticks. I didn't think of that."

Chapter Fifteen

On Sunday morning, Denzil's young apprentice, Brett and his girlfriend, Becky, called at Holly Cottage to meet Jamie and Mike; the four sat out on the lawn in the front garden chatting like lifelong friends and before Becky and Brett departed all had agreed to meet up again in the afternoon and spend time together on the beach.

Because the boys were unfamiliar with the area, Brett and Becky called again at the cottage in order to show them the quickest way to the sea. Having all the time in the world they then wandered slowly along the lanes and roads and Becky in particular pointed out places of interest. After passing by the Duck and Parrott they reached the first of several flights of steps that led down from the pavement onto the beach. Near to the steps was the slipway where lightweight vessels rested beneath a level area for storage of crab and lobster pots, dahns, nets, coils of rope and other fishing gear.

A fresh onshore wind blew from the south-east as they stepped down onto the beach and chose a patch of shingle free sand on which to place their belongings. After Jamie unzipped his rucksack he held up a lidded plastic box. "Granny insisted we bring something to eat and drink to make up for the calories burned while swimming. I hope you're both hungry because there's enough here to feed an army."

"Great minds think alike," Becky dropped a folded blanket onto the sand and pulled a box of sandwiches and slices of cake from her rucksack.

"Just as well I didn't think to bring anything then." To help Becky, Brett spread out the blanket on the sand and everyone placed their possessions around the edges to prevent the wind getting beneath it. They then removed the outer garments that covered their swimwear.

"How tall are you?" Becky asked as Mike peeled off his T shirt and jeans to reveal a pair of long, skinny legs.

"Five eleven."

"What! But you're only thirteen. Although I have to admit you look several years older."

"Mr tall, dark and handsome doesn't act it though," laughed Jamie.

"You're a fine one to talk," tutted Mike, "Don't forget I know you brought Rodney down here to Cornwall."

"Rodney?" Brett asked.

Mike smothered a smile. "He's Jamie's teddy bear."

Jamie blushed. "That's because he wanted to come and see Granny and Granddad. They bought him for me, you see, and Granny loves him. When I was little she used to make him talk and I believed every word he said."

"And how many years ago was that?" Becky was amused by the boy's banter.

"Ten," admitted Jamie, "It was for my third birthday."

"Are your parents tall?" Brett was keen to get back to a more serious topic.

"Dad is. In fact he was the same height as I am now when in his early teens but he didn't grow much after that. He's six one now so we reckon I'll be about the same."

"Must be nice to be tall," said Brett, wistfully, "I've been five nine for years and it's unlikely I'll grow any more now."

"You might be lucky," said Mike, kindly. "I'm told most people stop growing by the time they're in their late teens but others carry on into their early twenties."

"Yay! Thanks for that, Mike. I'm seventeen so there's hope for me yet."

The sea was a little rough due to the wind so they swam close to the shore and Brett, who was not a confident swimmer, paddled and poked around in rock pools near to the slipway. One by one they then made their way back to the blanket and ate their picnic lunches.

As they packed away the empty food containers, Dylan, the son of Gail and Robert Stevens, licensees of the Duck and Parrot, arrived on the beach. With him were newcomers to the Buttercup Field Estate, Libby and Luke Reynolds, both eager to learn the basics of surfing.

"Dylan makes it look so easy," said Brett, in awe.

"Well it can't be that difficult, can it?" Mike asked.

"Oh but it is. I've tried it and I was useless but then again I'm none too fond of getting my face wet which of course happens all the time if you keep falling off. Becky's quite good though, aren't you, Bex?"

"Not bad, but I'll never reach competition level."

Eventually, tired of sitting in the wind, they made their way back through the village towards Lady Fern Lane. As they walked along Smuggler's Lane and passed the junction with Glebe Road, Becky pointed to the first house in a row of semis. "That's where I live, along with Mum and Dad, of course."

"Nice," said Jamie, "and I like the idea of a wood nearby."

"It's the same wood that you can see from your grandparents' place and the stream that runs across their back garden part runs through the woods too. When I was much younger I'd spend ages in there with my friends climbing trees and making dens. It was great fun."

"Do you have any brothers or sisters?" Jamie asked.

"No, sadly not but I wish I had."

"You're lucky," said Mike, "I have a sister and she's a right pain. Ridiculously organised too so I get lots of 'why can't you be neat and tidy like your sister'."

"But they're right," said Jamie, "your room's a tip."

Becky smiled. "I can sympathise, Mike. My folks nag me too but I'm the outdoor type and there are far more interesting things to do than tidying my bedroom."

"So have you lived there long?" Jamie waved his hand towards Becky's home.

"We moved there about sixteen years ago when I was small. The house used to belong to the council but it was sold off like loads of others donkey's years ago. The bloke who first bought it had lived there forever. When he died he left it to a cousin or something like that, and Mum and Dad bought it off him." She laughed, "Would you believe, Mum fell for the place because there's a big Bramley apple tree in the back garden."

"I'd believe anything of parents," said Mike.

"So if you're seventeen you've lived in the village nearly all your life," calculated Jamie.

"Yes, and I don't think I'd want to live anywhere else. I might change my mind when I'm older though."

Mike nodded with approval. "Well, I think it must be cool living here. What with the sea, woods and dead bodies in cellars, there's lots going on."

Brett tutted. "Only one dead body in one cellar, thank goodness."

"Yeah, okay."

Jamie's curiosity was roused. "Can you two tell us anything about the bloke in the cellar? We'd love to know more and have asked my grandparents but they seem reluctant to discuss it with us."

Becky groaned.

"I was there when we found him," Brett spoke with pride, his initial shock long forgotten. "In fact it was me who pulled out the old rug that he was wrapped in."

"Yuck. Gross!" Mike muttered.

"I think we ought to find out what happened to the bloke, whatever he's called," said Jamie. "You know, pretend we're private investigators. Although if we do we'll have competition because I get the impression my grandparents and some old friends of theirs are doing the same and that's probably why they won't tell us much. If that's the case it might be useful though as we'll be able to snoop on their findings."

"I must admit I thought it'd be interesting when he was found," said Becky, "but now knowing that he's been dead for forever and the bloke who killed him most likely is too, I don't see the point."

"Well, I'm game," said Brett, ignoring his girlfriend, "although I won't have much time because Denzil has loads of work on. I can help in the evenings and at the weekends though."

"Great! That's settled then. We'll all be PIs." Jamie spoke with enthusiasm.

Mike shook his head. "It sounds like fun but I'm not really that keen. I mean, we might get into trouble."

Becky shifted her bag from one shoulder to the other. "As I said I'm not that keen either. I won't be able to be with you all of the time anyway because I work a couple of days a week at the garden centre. Which is probably just as well."

Having doubts, Mike attempted to change the subject and pointed out a distant building nestled in the hills. "What's that place?"

Becky's eyes followed the direction of his hand. "Oh that, that's Pendilly Cove Care Home. It used to be a hotel but changed usage after it was sold ten years or so ago. I know that because my aunt worked there when it was a hotel and my mum works there now it's a care home."

"So, is it a care home for old folks?" Jamie asked.

"Yes, and it's where the elderly lady now lives who your grandparents bought their house from. It's run by Jenny and Terry Carne. They're really nice. Dad was at school with Terry, so I know him quite well."

"I suppose everyone here knows everyone else," said Mike, "I mean, compared with a town the village is quite small, isn't it?"

"It's quite spread out and the population is roughly fifteen hundred so it's not that small," said Brett. "We studied the village and its population when I was at school."

"Hmm," Jamie shuffled his feet through loose stones on the side of the road. "So what are we going to do tomorrow?"

Becky's eyes shone. "I know. How about we borrow Dad's rowing boat and go for a paddle along the coast. He won't mind. In fact he'll be glad to see it used as he never has the time."

"Will we have to lug it down there from your place?" Jamie looked back along the road towards Becky's home.

"No it's already near the beach on the slipway. In fact we passed it a while back. It stays there right through the summer months unless there's a gale forecast and then in the winter Dad takes it up home."

"Ideal! A trip along the coast it is then," said Jamie, "if the sun shines it should be fun."

"Won't it be too windy though?" Mike was conscious of his ruffled hair.

"No, the wind will have gone by the time it's dark and although the water might be a bit choppy it'll be fine." Becky who was into gardening made a point of keeping up to date with weather conditions.

"Have you done any rowing before?" Brett asked.

"Yep, loads of it," said Mike. "I live near a river and Mum and Dad have a little boat moored at the bottom of our garden. Jamie and me have taken it out loads of times, haven't we, mate?"

"We have and we have the muscles to prove it." Jamie flexed his arms. "We both belong to a rowing club too so you've no need to worry about us. We'll do our fair share of the work."

"Are there any caves along this coast?" Mike asked.

Brett nodded. "Yep, there are and I know that because Dad used to go in them when he was younger. When the tide's out you can get to them by land from a cliff path leading down to a small cove. When the tide's in though you can only get to them by sea. Never really appealed to me as I'd be terrified of getting cut off by the tide and not being able to swim very well I'd not want to risk being unable to get back onto the coastal path."

Jamie's ears pricked up. "Yeah, I can see your point but I think that sounds fascinating and I'd love to have a poke around. I mean, that's what Cornwall is all about, isn't it? Secret passages and smuggling."

"And fishing, piskies and pirates," chuckled Mike, "especially pirates."

Brett pulled a face. "Pirates? What century are you living in?"

"Ah, don't mind us," said Jamie, "It's just last year our school did a production of The Pirates of Penzance and Mike and me were in the chorus. We loved it and have had a thing about pirates ever since. I must admit I was over the moon when Granny said we could come and visit them once they'd settled in. I mean, what better place to come for a holiday."

"Yes, but pirates." Brett rolled his eyes. "Each to his own, I suppose."

"Each to his own," teased Becky, "where on earth did you pick up an old fashioned phrase like that?"

"Would you believe old Nora? She often says it and the last time was when she heard the music I was listening to out in the back garden while sunbathing. She was getting her washing in at the time and leaned over the fence to comment. It was said in good humour though cos there's nothing mean about Nora."

"So what time shall we go tomorrow?" Jamie was keen to make plans.

"In the morning," said Becky, "around ten. It'll be high water then so easier to launch the boat."

Brett groaned. "Oh well, I won't be able to join you because I'll have to work of course, but I hope you have a great time."

Chapter Sixteen

As it turned out, Becky was also unable to join Jamie and Mike for a row along the coast. A work colleague had phoned in sick at the garden centre and her employer had asked if she would like to cover for the day. Needing the money, Becky was happy to oblige and after explaining her original plans to her employer, it was agreed that she'd start at eleven after she'd seen the boys off. So when they met on the beach at the pre-arranged time she told of her dilemma but said that her parents had agreed they could take the boat out on their own as they were both accomplished rowers but they must keep near to the shoreline and not go too far. She also warned them not to stay out too long for showers were expected later in the morning and they were likely to be heavy and prolonged.

The sea was still a little lumpy but not rough enough to be a threat and so the boys, thrilled to have earned the trust of Becky's parents, took the boat from the slipway and rowed along the coastline keeping as near to the shore as possible. Half a mile away from the village, Mike pointed towards the cliff base. "Do you think those dark patches might mean they're the entrances to caves? You know, the ones Brett's dad used to explore."

"Not possible to tell from here. Let's row over there and have a nose round. I mean, if they are it'd be daft not to investigate when we're so near."

"I'm more than game," enthused Mike. "It might be the only chance we get to explore and ideal too with no-one here to stop us."

With care they manoeuvred the boat towards the rocks, removed their trainers, rolled up the legs of their jeans, stepped into the waves and pulled the boat out of the water and onto a small stretch of sand and shingle. To their delight nearby was a small cavity in the cliff base that looked very much like the entrance to a cave. Knowing the boat would be safe as the tide was ebbing, they entered the cavity with fingers crossed and a little caution but found it was just a small chamber that led nowhere. After stepping back out into daylight they edged further along the cliff base towards a second opening where they paused and peered inside; to their unease it looked dark, gloomy, deep and cold. With neither boy prepared to admit to feeling nervous, they each put on a brave face, entered the cave and made their way across the uneven ground. In order to see where they were treading, Jamie flashed around the torchlight of his mobile phone. However, within minutes they came to a dead end.

"Oh dear," there was a hint of relief in Jamie's voice, "I really thought this might lead somewhere. Still never mind, let's try another one." He turned ready to retrace their steps.

"Hang on a minute," feeling his flesh creep, Mike was transfixed to the spot, "Flash your phone up on the ceiling again, Jamie. I'm sure I saw something up there."

With a frown, Jamie did as asked. In the beam of light, small creatures were visible hanging from the cave's ceiling. "Bats," he screeched, fear in his voice, "Hundreds of the little buggers. Let's get out of here."

"Are you sure they're bats?" Not convinced, Mike grabbed the cap from Jamie's head and threw it upwards to see if he could dislodge them. The cap however missed its target and disappeared over a ledge.

"You Muppet. That's my favourite hat." Jamie flashed the light towards the ledge. "I'll have to scramble up there now to see where it is."

"I'm sorry, mate. Here, let me climb up there. My legs are longer than yours."

"No, don't worry, I'll be fine." Looking for foot holds as he went, Jamie scrambled over a boulder and shone his phone light into the cavity over the ledge. "Wow! It opens into a larger space, Mike. I can't see my hat though so I'll climb over and take a proper look." Without hesitation he clambered through the space and dropped down onto the other side.

"Found it," he shouted, "and there are no bats in here, thank goodness."

"Is it worth me coming over? I mean is there anything there to see?" Mike's voice was tinged with excitement.

Jamie placed the cap back over his unruly mop of blond hair. "Not really worth it, just stones, stones and more stones. Oh hang on. Yes, there is something. How weird, it's an old hessian sack."

"A sack. Anything in it?"

"Don't know but it looks lumpy. Come and see."

Mike scrambled up onto the ledge and jumped down where he landed by Jamie's side. He looked at the sack. "Wonder why it's here. Shall we open it?"

"I don't know what to say." Jamie flashed around his torchlight looking for another way in. There was none. "It doesn't make sense. I mean, this place is tiny and the only way in here is the way we came over the ledge. So whoever the sack belongs to, well, he must have chucked it in here."

"Yes, but why?"

Jamie shrugged his shoulders. "No idea. Maybe he needed to hide it because someone was after him or maybe it's just rubbish."

"Don't be daft. No-one would go to the trouble of coming out here just to dump rubbish."

"No, I suppose not."

Mike prodded the sack with his foot. "Seems quite solid. It can't do any harm so let's have a look and see what's inside."

Jamie was hesitant. "No, I don't think we should."

"Why ever not?"

"Because it might contain drugs or guns even and if we open it and touch something our fingerprints will be on whatever."

"Drugs. Guns." Mike suddenly felt weak. "I hope you're joking."

"No, I'm not." Jamie knelt down and ran his hands over the sack. "I don't know what to think. There are all sorts of shapes in here and this feels like something round. A ball perhaps."

The colour drained from Mike's face. "Or a skull. I bet it's missing Maggie. You know, the woman we overheard your grandparents talking about who went missing during the war. I bet she's in there."

Jamie sprang back. "Really! Do you think so?"

"Well I don't know for sure but she might be."

"Yuck! That's grim and whatever we can't leave it here now you've said that and we certainly don't want to open it if Maggie's in there."

"So what shall we do?"

"Well I suppose we could go back and tell my grandparents what we've found and they can come and fetch it if they want, or better still we can take it back with us now and let them open it."

"I think taking it with us might be best as I'm curious to know what's in it," Mike walked around the sack weighing up its size, "Is it very heavy, do you think? Because we need to get it up the wall and over the ledge."

Jamie stepped forward and lifted the sack. "It is a bit but we'll be able to manage it between us."

Without too much exertion the boys were able to drag and push the sack over the ledge and into the larger part of the cave. As they carried it between them towards daylight, the bats, oblivious of the activity beneath them, remained in situ. However, when they stepped out onto the sand their hearts sank. The rain Becky had warned them about had begun and was already falling heavily.

With no choice other than to get back to dry land, they successfully placed the sack inside the boat and pushed the vessel out to sea. As they rowed back towards Trenwalloe Sands as fast as their arms would permit, the raindrops turned to hail and a flash of lightning sparked way out at sea. Drenched to the skin, they finally arrived back in the safety of the village where they pulled the boat up the slipway and secured it.

"We can't lug this all the way back to your grandparents' place," said Mike, as he struggled to push his wet feet into his wet trainers, "The sack's soaking wet now so will weigh more than ever."

Jamie tried to put on a brave face and then laughed. "No, no we won't have to. Remember, Grandma said she was going to meet her old friends at Dilly's place and apparently she lives somewhere along the seafront. I'll give Gran a ring."

After a brief call, Jamie shivering with cold, returned his phone into the pocket of his jeans and pointed to the top of a flight of steps. "It's up there somewhere. Lavender Cottage it's called. Gran said it's easy to recognise because there are lots of colourful flowers in the front garden."

When they reached the top of the steps they looked across the road and instantly saw the dahlias. Thankful the sack would soon no longer be their responsibility, holding one corner each they dragged it across the road and knocked on the door. Dilly, having been looking out for them, promptly answered and invited them inside where large towels waited. They were guided towards the glowing coke behind the grid of the Truburn which Dilly always kept alight even through the summer. When the boys were dry and dressed in clean clothes, with hot drinks in hand and their wet clothes transferred to a carrier bag, the ladies began to ask questions.

“So what have we here?” Kate asked, amused to see the boys dressed in Dilly’s jumpers and trousers.

Jamie, with prompting from Mike, told of the morning’s events.

“Oh bless you,” chuckled Dilly, “but I think it’s highly unlikely to be drugs or guns and certainly not Maggie Jones.” She rose from her chair and ran her hands over the side of the wet sack they had placed in Dilly’s plastic washing basket to prevent it soaking the fireside rug. “I see what you mean though. Something in here feels round.”

“It could be a skull,” reasoned Kate, “after all we don’t know what happened to Maggie and the account of her disappearance did sound fishy.”

Amelia chuckled. “Oh, I don’t think so,” her face then dropped, “but on the other hand, you could well be right.”

“Well, there’s only one way to find out. Dilly took a bread knife from the drawer in the sideboard and sawed through thick rope. When it gave way she turned the sack upside-down and tipped its contents into the washing basket. Out fell a black case covered in mildew, a leather-bound prayer book, a cricket bat, a table lamp with a rounded wooden base, a small painting and a cuckoo clock.

Chapter Seventeen

"Oh, so it's not Maggie Jones," Jamie plonked himself down in a vacant chair, clearly disappointed. Mike, however, looked relieved.

"No, it's not Maggie, and thank goodness for that," Dilly knelt down beside the sack's contents. "This is obviously the stuff that was taken from your place, Kate, back during the war years when Archie and Mavis Penrose had the tenancy but were away."

"I was thinking the same thing," said Kate.

Amelia agreed.

To prevent leaving fingerprints, Dilly pulled on a pair of rubber gloves and attempted to open the black case but the clasps had rusted. Not one to be out-done, she fetched a can of WD40 and sprayed it onto the rust. After leaving it for two minutes she tried again and all three clasps sprang open. Inside a gleaming trumpet was encased in rich blue velvet fabric. Dilly picked up the instrument. "Yes, definitely looks like we're right then because this must have belonged to poor Archie. Nora said something about him playing in the village's brass band. No doubt the same band that dear old Bert played in but several years later of course. How very sad."

"And the cuckoo clock," said Amelia, "although I think its days of singing are well and truly over."

Dilly picked up the prayer book. Its cover was damp but the inner pages were unharmed. Inside was the inscription, *To Mavis, wishing you a happy ninth birthday. Love from Mum and Dad.*

"Is that little picture of Trenwalloe Sands?" Jamie asked. "It looks like it is."

Dilly picked up the small brass frame, it was tarnished and the cardboard backing was damp but the picture itself, protected by glass, was not spoiled even though the glass was cracked. "Yes, I believe it is and it's a painting done in water colour." She looked closely at the signature, "Oh dear, that's so sad. The signature looks like A. Penrose so it was most likely done by Archie."

Confident as to where the contents of the sack had originated, Dilly rang Dotty and asked her to relay the news to Gerry on the off-chance the police might want to look into it further. Although she could see no reason why for even if they were able to get fingerprints from the items, after eighty years there would be no record of petty thieves in the database to find a match with.

Mike scowled. "What I want to know is, if all this stuff was nicked from Holly Cottage years and years ago, why did the thief chuck it away? I mean, why risk taking it in the first place if he didn't want it? It must be worth something so why not sell it or whatever?"

Kate shook her head. "I've no idea, Mike."

"Well if you ask me I should imagine it was stolen to cover up the fact that Mavis Penrose's crucifix and the rug were missing because they were buried along with Harold Jenkins in the cellar," Amelia reasoned. "I mean, whoever was responsible for Harold's death might have feared Mavis returning home to pick up any items she had left behind. And if several things were missing then she'd assume the place had been burgled and wouldn't think any more of it. On the other hand if just her cross and the rug were nowhere to be found, she'd have been puzzled."

"And we know that's more or less what happened," said Dilly, "Mavis herself didn't come back to collect the stuff though, instead she sent her brother and it was him who found some things were missing."

"Hmm, I suppose that makes sense," agreed Mike.

"It does but I don't see why whoever nicked the stuff went to all the trouble of hiding it in a cave in the first place," said Jamie. "Believe me it was tricky to get to where it was, so it would have been much easier to have just chucked it in the sea if it wasn't wanted."

Mike punched his friend's arm. "If he'd done that it might have got washed ashore, you numpty. Then if someone found it the folks back then would have put two and two together."

"Two and two together! What are you talking about?"

Kate patted her grandson's arm. "Mike's right, Jamie, because had the discarded sack been washed ashore and the items inside identified as belonging to the Penroses, then they'd have noticed that the rug and the cross were not amongst the items and wondered where they were."

Mike knelt down on the floor beside the sack's scattered contents. "So are you saying you really think this stuff was nicked by whoever did poor old Harold in?"

"Without doubt," Dilly was confident.

"Wow! That's cool." To cover his hands so as not to leave fingerprints, Mike pulled down the sleeves of the jumper he wore belonging to Dilly and picked up the table lamp, dirty and discoloured through the years. "And it must have been this we thought was old Maggie's head." As he ran his hand over the lamp's carved global base, something dropped from inside the shade onto other items in the washing basket. It was the letter 'M' on a silver chain.

Dilly picked it up. "M for Mavis, I assume."

"Or it could have fallen from the neck of whoever nicked this stuff," reasoned Jamie. "Someone like old Maggie perhaps."

The next morning, Jamie entered the kitchen at Holly Cottage for breakfast while Mike was in the shower. As he sat at the table and helped himself to a bowl of cereal he glanced up at the calendar hanging above the empty inglenook fireplace. "What's that picture of, Granny? It looks like a castle."

"It is. The calendar is of places in Cornwall and this is Saint Michael's Mount near Penzance." As Kate reached up for the calendar so Jamie could take a closer look, she gasped. "No! I don't believe it. It's back."

"What's back?"

"The outline of the cross." Kate then explained what she had been told by Elsie Mitchell the previous owner of Holly Cottage.

Jamie's eyes shone brightly. "So you think that cross is the outline of the crucifix found with old Harold?" Jamie stood up to take a closer look. "Wow! It has to be a sign."

"A sign?" Kate was confused.

"Yes, a sign from the other side. I reckon Harold's trying to tell you something, Granny."

Kate shuddered. "Oh dear. I hope not."

As Jamie poured milk onto his breakfast cereal, Mike entered the kitchen wearing shorts and a T shirt, his face pink from the shower, his dark hair wet and looking almost black. He pulled out a chair and sat down. "Please don't think I'm being nosy, Katie, but why are there two lumps of plaster on the landing window sill with scribbles on them?"

Kate explained.

"Wow," enthused Mike, "that's brill and it might make it easier to track down old Harold's killer."

"That's what we thought but sadly we've yet to come across anyone from back then with those initials and the same goes for someone called George."

Mike was full of confidence. "Leave it with us, Katie. We'll have a scout round the churchyard and see what we can find. I mean, they must be buried there somewhere."

"Hmm, maybe, but the vicar hasn't had much luck. Having said that he's only looked for the initials and for George in baptisms. It'd be a big job to check deaths as they could well be years apart or not even buried here."

Jamie, who had been very quiet suddenly spoke, "It's another sign, Granny. You finding those initials is another sign."

Shortly after breakfast, Jamie and Mike walked towards the village to Glebe Road where they hoped to find Becky at home so they could tell her of the latest developments. They found her outside cleaning windows; a chore she did to help her mother who had a full time job at the care home. While she finished the last of the windows, they told her of their discovery in one of the caves. Surprised and keen to hear more detail, she led them indoors where she put away the cleaning materials and poured three glasses of Coke. They took these into the back garden and drank them sitting on a bench beneath the Bramley apple tree. After Becky digested a more detailed account of the previous day, Jamie came up with a question.

"What I want to know is why my grandparents and their friends keep going on about old Harold's friends who were with him on the night before he died. I mean, they'll all be dead now, won't they, so what's the point? They obviously didn't kill him and they'd have been questioned by the coppers back then anyway, so surely instead they should be looking into any dodgy characters who were around in the olden days. You know petty thieves and what have you. People with the initials SC and AN too. Oh yes, and people called George. They're more likely to be involved and the plaster proves they were in the house at some point."

Becky finished her drink and placed the empty glass on the grass. "You've heard about the plaster chunks then."

"Yes, I spotted them earlier today and asked Katie about them." Mike turned to Jamie, "I can see what you mean about old Harold's friends but you've got to remember that when he went missing everyone assumed he'd done a runner so the coppers wouldn't have been too bothered. I mean, the only person who knew he was dead was the bloke who'd killed him."

"That's right, Mike," agreed Becky, "and by looking into Harold's family, Jamie, we've already traced the daughter of his sister, Grace. So if we can find any descendants of his friends too, there's a slim chance stories about that particular era might have been passed on through the generations. If so it could highlight any enemies Harold might have had or just reveal another version of what happened the night they all met up. Families do pass on stories especially when something a bit odd has happened."

Jamie frowned. "You mean, like instead of going home Harold might have planned to go off and meet someone. But his friends didn't want to let on for some reason or other in case it got him into trouble."

"Yes and that really is a possibility. You've got to remember the friends didn't know he was dead, so they would have expected him to come back at some point."

"Or," said Mike, his voice sinister, "your grandparents and their mates might think old Harold's friends bumped him off. I mean, they could have done, couldn't they?"

Becky shook her head. "No. I mean, why on earth would they have done that?"

As Jamie shrugged his shoulders they heard a door open and a soprano voice singing as the head and shoulders of a grey haired lady walked down the neighbouring garden. On hearing voices, the head turned and peeked over the fence. "Morning Bex. Beautiful day again."

"It is, Joy and far too nice to be stuck indoors."

Joy raised her thumb. "Should dry my sheets okay." She then resumed her singing and began to peg out her washing.

"Who's that?" Jamie asked.

"Joy Williams who would you believe is our next door neighbour. She's really sweet and lives alone having lost her husband a couple of years ago."

Mike tilted his head to one side. "She's got a nice voice and we know that song don't we, Jamie. It's from the Pirates of Penzance."

Jamie opened his mouth to start singing when an apple fell from the tree, bounced on his head and then rolled off into the grass.

"Blimey! Did you see that?" Jamie rubbed his head, "That'll probably leave a dent."

"Perhaps the tree's trying to tell you something," laughed Becky.

Jamie's eyes flashed. "Yes, of course, it'll be a sign."

Mike rolled his eyes. "Here we go again."

"Sign?" Becky was puzzled.

Mike answered quickly. "Jamie's great auntie something or other is as nutty as a fruitcake and she's always looking for signs and now it seems he's afflicted with the same nonsense too."

"It's not nonsense, Mike. Look at what happened yesterday. When you threw my hat at the bats something made it go over the ledge so we'd find the sack. It's all to do with a helping hand from above or wherever."

"Or perhaps Mike's just a rotten shot," laughed Becky.

"No I'm not, a gust of wind must have blown it off course."

"I'm only pulling your leg." Becky turned to Jamie, "So, how might the apple be a sign?"

"Well, umm, yes, I know, I know. The apple falling from the tree is like it did for that bloke. You know, the one who discovered the law of gravity."

"Isaac Newton," laughed Becky, "What's he got to do with any of this?"

"Well, it could be something as simple as the bloke who killed old Harold was called Isaac or Newton. Perhaps even Bramley or Apple."

"Okay, well I'll give you the benefit of the doubt and next time I see your gran I'll ask if any of the names they know have anything to do with Sir Isaac Newton and apples. Although I think at the moment the only names they have are Reynolds and Triggs."

"No, don't mention it to Granny," said Jamie, "because we want to solve the mystery ourselves. And the way I see it is, if one set of initials on the plaster was AN, then I bet the N stands for Newton."

Chapter Eighteen

On Monday morning, Gerry, as instructed by DS Simon Dawson, called at Lavender Cottage to collect the sack of supposedly stolen items. When asked, he told Dilly as a formality they would test things for fingerprints but thought that even if any traces were found they would not help solve the case simply because there was no database of petty criminals back then with which to find a match. Furthermore, whoever stole the objects was unlikely still to be living.

"Yes, that's what we thought. Shame really because all finding this stuff seems to have done is lead to yet another dead end."

"Looks that way," Gerry lifted the sack to test its weight, "Oh, it's lighter than I thought it would be."

"That's because I put it on the clothes horse to dry before I put the stuff back in it. It was raining when the boys brought it here, you see, so it got rather wet which made it weigh a lot more."

"I see," Gerry moved the sack towards the door. "By the way we have had one slight development. That being we've managed to track down the son of Archie and Mavis Penrose, the erstwhile tenants of Holly Cottage to whom we assume this stuff belonged."

Dilly perked up. "Really, I hadn't heard that. Dotty is slipping."

Gerry grinned. "No she's not, it's because I forgot to tell her. We only made contact yesterday."

"I see, so was he, the son, able to say anything useful?"

"No, sadly, I'm afraid not. Simon spoke to him on the phone and asked a few questions. He also mentioned this sack of stuff and asked if it was likely to have been taken from his home while the family were away. But the old boy was too young to know what the missing items were and he wasn't really interested. Hardly surprising, after all it was a life time ago. He did say though that if the stuff was proven to have belonged to his parents then whatever the things are he doesn't want them. He's in his nineties now and is housebound."

"What about his sister? Nora mentioned she was a twin."

"That's right, she was his twin and Simon asked after her but apparently she died two years ago."

"Oh dear. So what'll happen to the stuff the boys found?"

"We asked him that and he said give it all to the two lads that found it. So providing it's of no help, and we don't think it will be, I'll drop it off at Kate and Larry's place when forensics have done with it."

As Jamie and Mike finished their lunch and placed their rinsed plates in the dishwasher, Kate asked how they planned to spend the rest of the day. To her amusement they informed her they were going to the churchyard to find people with the initials SC and AN; and while there they'd also look for anyone called George. They refrained from mentioning they would also be looking for names such as Newton, Isaac, Bramley or anything else to do with apples.

Glad they would be out getting fresh air, Kate said that she was going to visit someone at the care home and then on the way back she'd pop in to see Dilly. She then added not to worry about being locked out because she would be back before Denzil and Brett finished work at five.

The churchyard was much larger than the boys had anticipated. In close vicinity to the old building, gravestones dated back several centuries and in some cases, pitted stones, covered in lichen were difficult to read.

"It's no good looking here anyway," reasoned Jamie, "these graves are much too old so let's look for some from the last century."

"That's what I was thinking and if old Harold died in 1943 we need to find graves of people from that year onwards."

Jamie scratched his head. "It won't help us by finding when people died though, will it. I mean, people die at all sorts of ages. What we're looking for are people with the right initials and blokes called George."

"True, we are, but at the same time if we spot headstones that say how old people were, we can do a calculation and work out if they'd have been twentyish during the war years. If so they might have been friends of old Harold."

"You're right, so let's look for gravestones from 1950 to the present day of people who would have been twentyish in the 1940s. There can't be that many surely, especially with the right initials."

After twenty minutes of scouring headstones they decided to abandon their search for the name George because of its frequent use and concentrate instead on names from the right era linked to apples or with the initials AN and SC.

"Ah, look at this," Mike waved his arms, "It's the grave of Gladys and Garth Reynolds who were the parents of Betty Reynolds."

"Yeah, but we already know about them." Nevertheless, Jamie crossed to Mike's side where he looked down on a double grave edged with black granite and filled with discoloured white granite chippings.

After reading the memorial they continued their search but after finding nothing relevant, both felt downhearted.

"We'd better check over there," Jamie pointed to several rows of small memorial stones close together, "I should imagine they'll be for the ashes of people who were cremated."

However the search once again proved fruitless.

"I give up," said Mike in disgust, "let's do something else."

"Like what?" Jamie wanted to continue but had to admit they would most likely be wasting their time.

"It's really warm today so let's go to the beach."

"Okay," reluctantly Jamie agreed.

As they made their way back along the path, Jamie grabbed Mike's arm. "Look, how did we miss that?" Tucked neatly beside a wooden bench stood a polished granite headstone. It read:

In loving memory of
Samuel Cowling
1922 – 1998
and his beloved wife
Annie Cowling
1925 – 2001
Together forever.
RIP

"Bingo," shouted Mike as he reached for his phone and took a picture, "That should impress the old folks. Let's go and show them now. Your gran said she was going to see Dilly after the care home so we'll be able to catch them both together."

"Yeah, and then we'll go and see Becky. We know she'll be home because she said she would be doing college course work today."

Kate's visit to Pendilly Care home, was because the previous evening she and Larry had decided to invite Elsie to see the house in which she had lived for sixty years. They hoped it might also jog her memory for some useful information she may have heard in the past that could help them establish the identity of Harold's elusive friends or better still, his enemies. When Kate arrived at the care home she was surprised to find Elsie in the residents' lounge sitting beside Mabel.

After greetings were expressed, Kate took Elsie's hand. "As I said the other day, the sitting room and kitchen are finished now and I'm pleased to add we've nearly finished decorating the bathroom too. What's more, the roses, your roses, are looking beautiful and the scent is out of this world. I think they appreciate the dry spell of weather we've had, although they didn't like the downpour the other day. Anyway, Larry and I were chatting last night and we wondered if you'd like to see the old place. We'll pick you up and take you out there and give you tea and cake as well."

"Ow, bless you. I'm overwhelmed and don't know what to say," tears filled Elsie's eyes. "Except I should like that very much."

"Good, that's settled then. We'll make it one day next week then the patio outside the French doors will be finished too. Do you have any preference as to which day it is?"

"No, every day is much the same here so I'll leave that up to you, but whenever it's to be you'll need to arrange it with Jenny and Terry, of course. It wouldn't do for us to go out gallivanting without them knowing."

"Not a problem. I'll have a chat with them before I leave."

"Would it be alright for Mabel to come too? I've told her all about my house, your house, and would love her to see it."

"Yes, the more the merrier," Kate turned to Mabel, "you'd be most welcome to come as well."

"Are you sure? I mean, I don't want to put you to any trouble, dear."

"It won't be any trouble at all. In fact we'd be honoured to entertain a marvel such as yourself."

Mabel chuckled. "Well, I've been called a few things in my life but never a marvel."

"In fact, why don't we make a proper day of it and ask your boyfriend if he'd like to join us as well." Kate cast her eyes across the room to where the elderly gentleman watched a garden makeover programme on the television.

"Ow, he'd like that," whispered Mabel, "Poor chap has no family now so seldom gets out or has any visitors."

"Oh dear, I'll slip over and ask him." As Kate stood, Elsie took her arm. "No, no, wait until his programme's done. It's his favourite and he hates to miss any of it."

On leaving the care home, Kate drove to Lavender Cottage to collect the wallflower plants which were ready to bed out and also to drop off the freshly laundered clothes Dilly had loaned to the boys after their seagoing soaking. Kate was not surprised to find Amelia and Dotty there also.

"Just in time," said Dilly, "we were about to have another cup of tea. I'm sure you'll join us."

As Dilly reached for the kettle there was a knock on the front door. "Hmm, who's that I wonder?"

"Probably Ivy," said Amelia, "then we'll all be here."

But it wasn't Ivy. Outside on the path stood Jamie and Mike looking very excited. "We've found something ever so interesting," blurted Mike, waving his phone.

"Really! You'd better come in then," she led them into the living room where Kate was surprised to see them. Without wasting time on social niceties, Mike showed her the screen of his phone.

"Good grief. Show that to the other ladies."

Dilly on seeing it first, gasped. "Samuel Cowling and his wife Annie. Well done boys. It looks like you've solved the mystery of the scribblings on the wall."

"That's what we think," Mike passed his phone to Amelia and Dotty.

"We looked for Georges too," gabbled Jamie, "but there were millions so we gave up."

Kate smiled, amused by her grandson's wild exaggeration. "I'm not surprised there are a lot. George has always been a very popular name."

"Would you boys like a drink? We were just about to have tea but I've orange juice if you prefer."

Jamie shook his head. "Thanks but we won't stop because we want to get off to Glebe Road to show Becky what we've found."

"Of course. Off you go then."

After the boys left Dilly once again reached for the kettle but just as before there was a knock on the door.

Kate laughed. "Probably will be Ivy this time."

But again it wasn't Ivy. Outside on the path stood someone with whom Dilly was not acquainted.

"Ms Granger?" The stranger asked.

Dilly nodded, "Yes."

"I'm Miss Claudia Howard. Headmistress of the village school. I wonder, is Mrs Greenwood here?"

"Yes, yes she is. Do come in."

"You have a visitor, Kate," Dilly, overwhelmed with curiosity, followed the headmistress into the sitting room and closed the door, "Would you like a cup of tea, Miss Howard? We were just about to have one."

"That would be lovely, thank you."

Amelia patted the seat of the chair at her side. "Come and sit down, Miss Howard."

"How did you know I was here?" Kate, having never met or even clapped eyes on the headmistress before, was puzzled.

"Detective work," she chuckled. "I've actually been all round the houses, so to speak. First I went to the vicarage to see Peter but there was no-one in. I then went to Holly Cottage where Denzil was supervising the unloading of paving slabs from a lorry. He told me your husband was out on a job and that you'd gone to see Elsie Mitchell at Pendilly Care Home. I asked if he knew when you'd be back and he said probably not for ages because after the care home visit you were going to call in here to pick up some plants."

"Oh, good old Denzil. I wasn't sure if he was listening when I told him of our plans for the day but clearly he was." Kate frowned, "But why did you want to see me?"

"Well actually it was Peter I was trying to find because of a little chat we had the other day. As it is, what I wanted to say to him might be of interest to you all. You see, Peter and I talked briefly about the unfortunate discovery in your cellar, Mrs Greenwood, and I offered to look into old pupil records for contemporaries of Harold Jenkins who Peter believes would have been born in the early nineteen twenties."

Kate's face lit up. "Really. The subject of contacting you was brought up at a gathering at the vicarage but it was agreed it would be unacceptable to bother you during the school holiday."

"So Peter said, bless him, but I'm more than happy to help. In fact I have a list of names for that period with me now." She took a sheet of paper from her handbag and handed it to Kate.

Dilly, who had made the tea at her fastest rate ever, quickly handed out the mugs and then sat down to hear the details.

Kate looked at the list. "It might be better if you explained it to us, Miss Howard."

"Of course. I'll be happy to do that but please call me Claudia."

Kate chuckled. "And please call me Kate."

"And me Dilly."

"And you're Amelia," said Claudia, "I've seen you around with Ernie but have never been close enough to introduce myself."

"You know Ernie?" Amelia was surprised.

"Yes, I saw him out picking elderberries near to where I live one day and we got chatting. I hear he makes wine."

"Yes, yes he does and very nice it is too."

"So I've heard from several people." Claudia looked at Dotty, "I don't think I know you, dear, but perhaps I should because you're young enough for me to have taught you."

"Thank you for the compliment but no you didn't teach me because I'm from up-country and went to school there. I've been here for about five years now."

"Ah, that explains it. And your name is?"

"Dotty, Dotty Gibson."

"Dilly and Dotty. Wonderful."

"So whose names are on the list? We're itching to know." Amelia was feeling impatient.

"And so you shall." Claudia took a pair of reading glasses from her bag, put them on and glanced at the sheet of paper in her hand, "Well, firstly I looked for Harold Jenkins. He obviously wasn't born in the village because he didn't start school here until 1929 when he was nine years old so I assume that's the year the family took over the pub."

Three heads nodded sagely as they absorbed the facts.

"Right, so having established the year of Harold's birth as 1920 I looked for contemporaries of his. There are several but not many as, you understand, the village was much smaller then and so were school numbers. Anyway, there were two other boys of the same age. Arthur Nicholas born in 1920 and George Polkinghorne also born in 1920. George started school in 1925 when he would have been five years old. Arthur started in 1928 when he was eight so I assume like the Jenkins that his family moved to the village in the year he started school. There is also another boy who was a little younger, Samuel Cowling born in 1922." Claudia paused to turn over the sheet of paper, "There are also four girls. Betty Reynolds born in 1921. Sarah Cooper born in 1921, Amabella Triggs born in 1921 and Margaret Jones, a little younger, born in 1923. Sarah, Amabella and Betty started school in 1926 at the age of five and Margaret in 1928."

"Amabella," said Dotty, "are you sure that's right? We thought because her baptism entry was smudged, that of the three possibilities it was most likely her name would be Arabella or Annabella and not the unusual, Amabella."

"Well, that's what it says and the writing is very neat and clear." Claudia smiled, "I think it's rather charming and I know the Cornish do like to use unusual names."

Dilly nodded. "I agree with Dotty because I'd thought the same. And Margaret Jones must be Maggie Jones who disappeared shortly after Harold went missing."

"Yes, of course," said Dotty, "Well spotted, Dilly. And going back to the Jenkins, Claudia. Is there any mention of Harold's sister, Grace?"

"And Maggie's brother, Patrick?" Dilly added.

"Yes, but they were younger. Grace born in 1925 and Patrick Jones in 1926. Both started school at the age of five."

"May I look at the list please?"

"Of course." Claudia passed the sheet of paper to Dotty.

"Well we know Grace wasn't one of the young people out with Harold on his last night and back then Patrick would have been just seventeen so I think we can rule him out too."

"So who does that leave?" Dilly tried to recall the names.

"George Polkinghorne, Arthur Nicholas, Samuel Cowling, Maggie Jones, Betty Reynolds, Amabella Triggs and Sarah Cooper."

Dilly frowned. "Polkinghorne. Why do I know that name? I'm sure I've seen it somewhere."

"You have," said Dotty, "there's a plaque above the door leading into the sports room at the Duck and Parrot. The pub's freehold and in the early twentieth century, Henry Polkinghorne made a generous donation to the then licensees in order for them to create a sports area. The plaque is in recognition of that."

"Ah yes, I remember reading it now. So might the Henry in question be the father of George Polkinghorne, I wonder."

"Most likely," agreed Dotty, "but even if he was it doesn't help, does it? I mean, we already know George is or was the same age as Harold Jenkins so the name of his father is irrelevant."

"Oh dear. Yes, you're quite right."

Amelia finished her tea and over Kate's shoulder glanced through Claudia's list. "I must be getting old. Seeing all those dates is making my brain hurt."

Dilly patted her friend's arm. "Well don't let them. The dates don't matter anyway It's the names that are important and any of the six could have been friends with Harold and with him on the night before he disappeared."

"So how do we find out what happened to them?" Kate asked.

"Nora," suggested Dotty. "Now that we have names, she might be able to fill us in with more details."

"Only if they remained in the village," reasoned Amelia. "She wasn't born until 1932 so she'd have only been tiny when they left school."

Amelia felt a headache coming on. "Let's sleep on it and see what we think tomorrow."

“Dilly agreed. “Good idea, but I’ll ring Ivy later and tell her the names we have, and then when next at the vicarage she can ask Peter to check marriages and burials to see if he can find a match.”

Dotty took out her phone. “Pass me the list please, Kate, then I can take a picture of the names and show them to Gerry and Robin.”

“Good thinking and when you’ve done that I’ll do the same for Larry.” Kate handed the sheet of paper to Dotty and then searched through her handbag for her own phone.

“Great idea, and I’ll do the same to show to Ernie.”

After all had taken pictures, Amelia looked again at the names. “Oh my goodness. I’ve just spotted something but it might be insignificant after what the boys found today.”

Dilly frowned. “What do you mean?”

“The writing on your wall, Kate. *SC loves AN*. Well, here we have two more names that match. Sarah Cooper and Arthur Nicholas.”

“Of course. Well spotted, Amelia. But I wonder which one is right. Is SC a female called Sarah Cooper or a male called Samuel Cowling.”

“And I’ve just thought of something else,” said Dotty, “Could, I wonder, George Polkinghorne be the Georgie mentioned in the, *I love Georgie* scribbling.”

Chapter Nineteen

Jamie and Mike, unaware of the latest developments at Lavender Cottage, noticed the petite figure of a woman several yards ahead of them as they made their way to see Becky.

"I reckon that's old Joy," said Jamie, wagging his finger. "You know, Becky's next door neighbour and by the way she's walking I'd say her bags are heavy. Let's go and help her."

The boys ran along the road and when they caught up with Joy they each offered to carry her shopping bags. She seemed a little hesitant until she realised who they were. "Oh, I know who you are now. You're Becky's friends, aren't you?"

"Yes, and we're going to see her now so we'll be going your way."

"Well thank you very much," she handed her bags to the boys who took one each. "I only popped out for a few things but they had my favourite soup on offer so I bought twelve tins, which along with milk, a jar of marmalade, frozen peas, a bag of spuds and two bottles of wine, made the bags bloomin' heavy. Heavy for me anyway, but then my arms aren't as strong as they used to be."

"Lucky we came along then and are able to help. But then that's the way we were both brought up, isn't it, Jamie? To help people whenever we can, I mean."

"And you're both a credit to your parents. I don't think I've seen you before though. Well not until I saw you with Bex the other day. Are you new to the village?"

"No, we're on holiday," said Jamie. "Mike and I are best friends and we're staying with my grandparents for a while before we go back to school in September."

"I see. So where do your grandparents live?"

"Holly Cottage in Lady Fern Lane."

"Well fancy that. You'll be near Denzil's place then. Denzil's father and my late husband were cousins. Something like that anyway."

"Small world," said Mike.

"It certainly is," Joy turned to Jamie, "So it must be your grandparents who found Harold Jenkins. Everyone's talking about it."

"That's right. Did you know him?"

Joy threw back her head and laughed. "How old do you think I am?"

"Duh," said Mike, "Old Harold's been dead for eighty years, so for this good lady to have known him she'd have to be ancient."

"Correct, and for the record, I'm seventy-three."

As they reached Becky's gate, Joy took her bags. "I can manage this last bit but thank you very much for your help and our little chat. I really enjoyed it."

They found Becky sitting on the lawn beside a pond in the front garden, a book in her hands and a bag of toffees by her side.

"I thought you were supposed to be doing course work today," Mike called over the garden gate.

"Oh, I finished that ages ago," she laid the book down on the grass, "so what brings you two here?"

Mike held up his phone. "We've something to show you. Is it alright if we come in?"

"Of course."

They quickly unlatched the gate and stepped onto the lawn where Mike knelt down by Becky's side and handed her his phone with the picture taken in the churchyard. It took a minute or two for the significance to click. "Oh, I get it. Samuel Cowling could well be the SC whose initials were scribbled on Kate and Larry's wall."

"Exactly," Jamie sat down on the grass, "and his wife Annie could well be the A in the AN initials."

Becky handed the phone back to Mike. "But does it have any bearing on the case, do you think?"

"Well, we have a theory," said Jamie, with pride, "we discussed it before walking over here, you see."

"And…?"

"Our theory is that this Annie might once have been drop-dead gorgeous and her bloke Samuel might have been real jealous of other blokes chasing after her. So we think it's possible that one of the blokes who really liked her might have been old Harold, and when he came home on leave, Samuel might have been so envious that he decided to get rid of him and lured him to Holly Cottage which was of course empty. And there in the kitchen he bumped old Harold off and the rest as they say is history."

Becky tried not to laugh. "Hmm, feasible I suppose, Jamie, but there are rather a lot of 'might haves' in your theory and it does seem a little far-fetched."

"Ah yes, but as some bloke once said, truth is stranger than fiction."

After breakfast the following morning, Robin informed Gerry that he was popping down to Penzance for a couple of days to visit his widowed aunt; something he had promised his parents he would do when he'd told them of his planned trip to Cornwall. Having already phoned her, his aunt was expecting him and to make a change he planned to travel down by train.

Aunt Beattie was his father's half-sister and Robin had not seen her since she visited his parents a few years before.

He was also curious to see Penzance, a town his aunt had made her home in 1989 and of which she spoke with love and affection.

Gerry agreed it was a good idea and offered to drop Robin off at the railway station in St Austell before he went on to work.

Meanwhile, at his home on the Buttercup Field Estate, Orville was contemplating trimming his privet hedge when his doorbell rang. On answering he found Libby Reynolds, one of his new neighbours looking distressed and was concerned. "Are you alright?" he asked, even though it was clear that she wasn't.

"Not really and I don't know who to turn to but you were so kind when you welcomed us to the village and well, I thought I'd ask you for advice. I can't go to the police, you see, and Luke's at work."

"Police?" Orville opened the door wide. "You'd better come on in and tell me what the problem is."

After he'd made her a coffee and told her not to worry, Libby explained her dilemma. "On the doormat this morning I found a nasty letter. It didn't come with the post because there's no stamp on the envelope so I assume someone delivered it by hand. Anyway, the letter accuses Luke's great grandmother of murdering someone and the sender said if we don't leave ten thousand pounds in a soon-to-be-designated place then he'll report it to the police and we'll both lose our jobs. I've not told Luke because as I said he's at work. I don't know what to do though. It doesn't make sense. According to the letter, the bloke Luke's great grandmother murdered was called Harold Jenkins, whoever he might be, or have been if he's dead."

"Harold Jenkins," Orville was taken aback.

"Do you know of him then?"

"I certainly do." Orville then explained about Harold having been found in the cellar of a cottage along Lady Fern Lane and of the findings made by a small group of his friends.

"I see. So whoever sent this letter must think Luke's great grandma was this Betty Reynolds you've just mentioned." She suddenly looked relieved. "Silly sod. Luke and me have studied both our families' history and I know for a fact that his great grandparents on the Reynolds side of his family were James Reynolds and Catherine Reynolds nee Browning. Furthermore, neither of them came from Cornwall. Both were born and bred in Preston."

Orville smiled. "In which case you've absolutely nothing to worry about. Someone around here is obviously trying it on. The discovery of Harold Jenkins is common knowledge in the village and so whoever wrote the letter is clearly none too bright and will be hedging his bets on the off-chance you might be related. As you say - silly sod - because even if Luke was a descendant he'd not be guilty of anything and there's no proof that Betty Reynolds was a friend of Harold's anyway, let alone proof of her being in any way linked to his death."

"So what shall I do?"

"Do you have the letter with you?"

"Yes," she took it from her pocket and handed it to Orville. He read it through and then chuckled.

"Hmm, spelling's clearly not one of his skills," Orville stood up. "Do you have to be at work any time soon?"

"No, I have the day off."

"Good, in that case I suggest you take this to the police. You've done nothing wrong, Libby, but whoever sent it has. He's a fraudster and a blackmailer."

"Okay," she seemed hesitant.

"If you'll permit me I'll drive you there. I know several of the local coppers and I'm sure they'll be interested to hear your story, and see the letter."

In the back garden of Holly Cottage, Kate and the boys who had volunteered, began the process of digging an area to widen the stream to create a small pond. Shortly after they began, as pre-arranged, Becky called round to help as she was particularly interested in aquatic plants. With her she brought a bag full of windfalls from the family's Bramley apple tree.

Kate took the offered bag with gratitude. "Wonderful. Do thank your mum for me and assure her they'll not go to waste. In fact I shall go blackberrying this afternoon and make a blackberry and apple crumble for dinner tonight. That's if we get this pond sorted today."

"I'm glad you're pleased and if you can make use of them I'll bring you another bag before long because we always have far more than we can use. I'll bring some aquatic plants too. The ones in the pond I made for Mum and Dad need thinning so it'll be the ideal opportunity."

Kate gave Becky a hug. "Wonderful and thank you in advance."

"Are we going to put fish in this pond when it's done?" Mike asked.

"I'd love to say yes," Kate smiled, "but I think they might find their way out and swim off down the stream."

"Duh," Jamie punched his friend's arm playfully.

Mike was puzzled. "Okay, yes of course, I didn't think of that but if you're going to have plants in it then surely they'll float away."

"No, because they'll be in pots and away from the flow of the stream," reasoned Becky. "We'll weigh them down with pebbles as well to make them secure until they get bedded in."

"And it won't be a problem anyway," said Kate, "because the stream has a gentle flow."

As they worked, Becky asked if there had been any further developments in the Harold Jenkins' case other than the boys finding a gravestone with a possible match to the mysterious initials.

"Yes and no," Kate stopped digging and rested her hands on the handle of the spade. "Claudia Howard paid us a visit yesterday while we were all at Lavender Cottage. With her she had a list of pupils who would have been contemporaries of Harold's back in their school days. We're hoping the vicar might be able to trace marriages or burials for some of them but we'll leave it for a couple of days before asking because with Sunday coming up he may well be preparing sermons and what have you for the services he takes. Failing that it'll be back to see Nora."

"Really! Jamie and Mike didn't tell me about Miss Howard's visit when they came to see me yesterday."

"That's because she called round after we found the initials," said Jamie, "so we didn't know 'til we got back here."

"Oh, I see. Miss Howard's really nice, isn't she?"

"Yes, we thought so. In fact we all said after she'd gone that we'd like to know her better."

Becky pulled a pair of gardening gloves from her pocket and picked up a spade. "I wonder if I can help you with the names. I've lived here all my life so some might sound familiar. Do you remember what any of them are?"

"Well the one that jumps out is George Polkinghorne. Simply because I've never come across that surname before, although according to Dotty, a Henry Polkinghorne donated money to the pub for a sports room and we assume he'd have been George's dad. Apparently there's a plaque to commemorate this over the sports room door. I've not seen it but will look out for it next time I'm in there."

"Really? Can't say that I've seen it either but then I don't go in the pub very often, so next one please."

"Well, there's Reynolds. Betty Reynolds, but the vicar was able to help us there a bit because he'd seen a record of her baptism. Having said that, we've no idea what happened to her but we do know that her parents remained in the village and are buried here."

"Okay. Are there any more?"

"Amabella Triggs, but we don't know what became of her either. Then there's someone called something or other Cooper. Yes, it's another girl and her name begins with the letter S. Yes, that's it. Her name's Sarah, Sarah Cooper. Which of course is interesting because it matches the initials SC found on our old wall."

Becky smiled. "Ah yes, and those initials also match Samuel Cowling who the boys found in the graveyard."

Kate smiled. "They do, and I daresay if we were able to dig deep we'd find several people with the same initials over the years. But they'd be of no use anyway as regards the death of Harold unless they were from the right era."

"And I assume Samuel Cowling is on Miss Howard's list."

"Correct."

"So are there any more names?"

"Umm, I'm trying to think. Yes I know, Jones, Maggie Jones but we already know she disappeared without trace shortly after Harold went missing. There was also Harold's sister, Grace, of course and Maggie's brother, Patrick." Kate frowned, "There is one other lad. Yes, yes, I remember, it was Nicholas, Arthur Nicholas which of course is another match with the scribbled initials AN."

Becky stopped digging. "Nicholas, yes, I know that name. When I was little Mum and Dad would occasionally mention a Mr Nicholas and I assumed it was his Christian name. It wasn't until I was a bit older that I realised Nicholas was his surname."

"What can you tell me about him? Where did he live and was his name Arthur?"

"I don't know whether or not he was called Arthur. I never knew him because he died sixteen years ago when I'd have been just one, but I do know where he lived. It was in Glebe Road in a house that used to belong to the council which he bought years and years ago when houses were sold off to their tenants. He lived there for the rest of his life and when he died the house went to a cousin or something like that. The cousin or whatever then put it up for sale and it was bought by Mum and Dad."

Chapter Twenty

Two days later in the early evening, Robin arrived back at Trenwalloe Sands having taken a taxi from St Austell following the visit to his Aunt Beattie in Penzance. Knowing that Gerry would still be at work he sent him a text to say that he was back in the village and was popping into the pub for a quick pint. After buying a drink he cast his eyes around; no-one he knew was in and after catching the eye of a lone drinker he ended up chatting to the young man who was propping up the bar.

After a brief dialogue he established the stranger's name was Matt and that he was touring the southern half of the country on foot by way of the coastal path.

When asked, Robin told Matt that he was a novelist and part-time barman up country but knowing not everyone was a fan of the police he decided against adding that he had previously been in the Force. Matt seemed impressed that Robin was an author albeit almost unknown, and said that he was a self-employed plumber and it was because he earned well that he was able to afford to take time out to achieve his lifelong ambition of walking part of the coastal path.

An hour later Gerry entered the Duck and Parrot. As he approached the bar, the landlord greeted him warmly.

Realising Gerry was the friend Robin had been waiting for, Matt quickly finished his drink and excused himself saying something about meeting someone and not wanting to be late.

"So has anything exciting happened while I've been away?" Robin asked as Robert passed Gerry his pint.

"Well, the ladies had a visit from the headmistress who gave them a list of names so that's caused a bit of excitement. Having said that I think it was before you went away so you already know."

"It was and I do. Dotty showed me the list of names on her phone."

"Of course, yes, she showed me too," Gerry pulled up a stool and sat down beside Robin, "So who was that chap you were talking to?"

"A plumber from somewhere up the line who's walking the southern half of the coastal path. He's called Matt. He's staying here at the pub for a few days and seems a nice enough bloke."

"Walking the coastal path, eh. Well rather him than me. It's pretty treacherous in places especially down near Land's End."

Both men turned their heads towards the entrance as the door opened and Orville walked in with retired fisherman, Jim Blake, a fellow member of the Trenwalloe Sands Male Voice Choir.

"Any luck with finding out who sent the message to Libby and Luke?" Orville asked as he bought drinks at the bar.

Gerry shook his head. "There's been no follow up instructions so we think it might have been kids. The writing was pretty juvenile and there were several spelling mistakes. Mind you, they could have been deliberate to disguise someone's natural hand."

"Kids! Oh dear," tutted Orville, "I hope it's not Kate and Larry's grandson and his mate. I know they're interested in the case."

"No, I think that's highly unlikely. They strike me as being good lads and don't forget they found the sack of stolen goods and handed it over. I know young Jamie's cheeky but neither are dishonest."

Orville nodded. "Yes, I have to agree."

"What's all this about?" Robin asked.

Gerry explained.

"I see. Sounds a bit odd though. I mean, the new folks only moved in recently so surely not many people know their names let alone where they live."

"That's a good point," agreed Gerry, "but they are trying to socialise by coming in here frequently. They're in with the surfing crowd too and have joined various organisations. In fact they're so keen to get to know everyone they've even been to church."

"Yes, you've got to hand it to them. They're doing their best to fit in," said Orville, "and as for people knowing their name, well, news around here travels pretty fast and people are always curious to find out all they can about new folks."

The next day, having washed the breakfast dishes and dusted the furniture, Dilly sat down to take up the hem of new curtains she had purchased for her two bedroom windows. As she finished the first one and folded it, there was a knock on the door. Dilly answered to find a very excited Dotty dressed in her jogging clothes hopping from foot to foot.

"Have you heard?" Dotty asked.

"Heard what?"

"About the murder?"

"Murder! Good heavens, no." Dilly stepped aside, "You'd better come in."

"Thanks." Dotty closed the front door and followed Dilly into the living room. "I've only just heard myself. You see, after I'd been out jogging I popped in the shop for milk before going home and everyone in there was talking about it. Apparently the victim was some bloke staying at the pub. He only arrived a few days ago and was booked in for six nights and now he's dead."

"Oh dear. So what happened?"

"Someone duffed him up and nicked his wallet."

"While he was in the pub?"

"No, no, he was in the churchyard of all places. He was found there first thing this morning by someone who'd gone there to lay flowers or something like that." Dotty placed her hands on her lap and gazed into space, "I don't expect it's of any significance. In fact I'm sure it's just a coincidence, but it was Gladys and Garth Reynolds' grave he was found on. Face down in the granite chippings apparently."

Gladys and Garth. Aren't they the parents of Betty Reynolds?"

"Yes, they are."

Dilly held up her hand. "Don't say anymore for now, Dotty. I must give Amelia a buzz because she'll want to hear this."

Amelia was there before Dilly had a chance to return her phone to its place on the sideboard. When all were seated, Dotty brought Amelia up to date and then continued. "Well, according to the gossips in the shop, the bloke had been badly beaten and on the back of his head was a nasty gash so it's assumed that was the cause of death. Needless to say I'll know more when I've had a chance to speak to Gerry."

"You've not done so yet then," said Amelia.

"No, when I heard I came straight round here. I even forgot to get some milk so I must do that on my way home. Anyway, it'd be unfair to bother Gerry while he's working. I mean, they must all be involved down at the station."

Dilly stood up. "I think this calls for lubrication. Tea or coffee, ladies?"

Both asked for coffee. As Dilly reached for the kettle, there was another knock on the door. Outside stood Ivy.

"Have you heard the news?" Ivy, out of breath, gratefully accepted the invitation to step inside and after closing the front door Dilly led her into the sitting room. "If your news is what I think it is then, yes, we have. In fact we were just talking about it. Will you join us for coffee?"

"Yes please."

While Dilly made the coffee, Dotty repeated the details as she knew them.

"You've not heard who he is then?" Ivy asked.

Dilly handed out the mugs. "Well no, but then we'd not know him if he's a visitor staying at the pub."

"Well, yes, he is. But there's more to it than that. You see, I've just heard his name straight from the horse's mouth. The horse being Jim Blake who found him this morning when he went to put flowers on his mum's grave, it being the anniversary of her death."

"And?" said Dilly.

"Jim recognised him because he'd chatted to him in the pub yesterday lunchtime. He'd gone in for his lunch you see because Susan was out for the day and he can't even boil an egg. Anyway, the bloke's a plumber who's taking time out from work to walk along the coastal path. The significant thing though is that the hiker's name is Matthew Polkinghorne."

Dilly gasped. "Polkinghorne! Are you sure, Ivy?"

"Yes, because being old school and very chatty, Jim introduced himself as James Blake, retired fisherman who was best known as Jim. In return the bloke said he was Matthew Polkinghorne, a plumber and fresh air fanatic who loved hiking who was best known as Matt."

Dotty's hand suddenly flew to her mouth. "Oh, my goodness. I've just realised something. Gerry mentioned last night that Robin was chatting to a bloke in the pub before he met up with him after he'd finished work. I wasn't really listening but I recall him saying something about the bloke was walking the coastal path. I asked him if it was for charity, you see, and he said he had no idea. It has to be the same person."

"Hmm, might be worth questioning young Robin then," said Ivy.

"I agree," mused Dotty, "and if this Matt's name really is Polkinghorne, then there has to be a connection between him and Harold Jenkins."

"Not necessarily," reasoned Amelia, "but it does seem odd that the newly arrived young couple called Reynolds have been blackmailed and now someone called Polkinghorne is dead, and not just dead but murdered."

After digesting information received and wanting to know more, Dilly suggested they meet up the following evening to discuss the latest developments. All three visitors readily agreed. Hence with relevant documents, notes and thoughts on slips of paper and with ideas churning through their minds, Amelia, Ernie, Dilly, Orville, Ivy, Dotty, Robin, Kate and Larry all met up at the Duck and Parrot to chew over the latest news. Jamie and Mike stayed at Holly Cottage with Brett and Becky for company where the four planned to play video games.

The choice of venue was because they hoped the deceased having booked accommodation there, might enable them to glean information from anyone who had spoken to him, or of any new developments. After asking the landlord's permission, the party pushed two tables together.

"No Freddie and Max this evening?" Ernie asked as he took a seat.

Dilly closed her handbag having pulled out her debit card. "It's Helen's birthday so they've taken her out for a meal. She said they could cancel but Max wouldn't hear of it. Now, drinks are on me so what would everyone like?"

Amelia stood up. "I'll give you a hand, Dilly."

"Who's Helen?" Kate asked Dotty, who was sitting by her side.

"Max's mum. She's a widow and doesn't get out much."

"Oh, I see. And what about your policeman boyfriend. Isn't he coming either?"

"He's working at the moment but might join us later."

When all had drinks and Robin had recounted his brief exchange of words with the deceased, Ivy asked the question on everyone's lips. "Right, do we think Matthew Polkinghorne is, or should I say was, related to George Polkinghorne who may or may not have been one of the young people with Harold Jenkins on the night before he disappeared?"

"It's a good question," agreed Orville, "but if he is or was, what's the significance?"

Dilly tutted. "The significance is, my dear Orville, that if the late Matthew was a descendant or distant relative of George from backalong, then having heard of Harold's discovery, he might have been here to look into any known facts about his grandfather, great uncle or whatever. The reason being he'd want to find out what we know about the case and if his ancestor is a suspect. Something like that."

Orville frowned "But to do that he'd need to know about the body's discovery and if this Matt bloke came from up-country, then how would he know that?"

"Stop putting spokes in the wheel, Orville King," growled Dilly, "He could quite easily have heard about it during his travels, or as things are today, he might have read about it on social media."

"Exactly," said Amelia, "and if there is a link between Matthew and George then the fact that poor Matt is now dead must surely indicate that he knew something about the goings on back in 1943."

"Such as?" Orville enjoyed playing devil's advocate.

Dotty tutted. "Such as, Orville, someone who's maybe a descendant of Harold's killer, got wind of Matt being a Polkinghorne and knew there was a chance he'd spill the beans, thus causing that someone to want him silenced - permanently."

"Absolutely," agreed Dilly, "and then of course there's the blackmail letter sent to your new neighbours Libby and Luke. Mark my word. Somewhere someone is scared the truth might come out."

"What do the police think, Dotty?" Ivy asked, "I assume you've talked about it with Gerry."

"Gerry won't say much other than they think it was robbery."

"But you don't need to murder someone to nick their wallet," reasoned Orville.

"Hmm, maybe not," agreed Ernie. "On the other hand, perhaps this Matthew Polkinghorne recognised his attacker."

"Possible, I suppose," agreed Kate, "but if that's the case and the attacker knew his victim then surely he would have worn a mask or whatever."

"Well, for what my opinion is worth I don't think it was a bungled robbery," said Larry, "I know his wallet was taken but that might have been to make it look like robbery."

Kate wasn't convinced. "Maybe, but I think it's worth remembering that Matthew was walking the coastal path, so if he was raising money en route he would have paid it into a bank account whenever he got the chance. Meanwhile there could have been a hefty amount still in his wallet."

Dotty addressed Robin. "You spoke to him, Rob. Was he raising money do you think?"

"No, I'm sure he wasn't. At least that's the impression I got. I mean, for a start he was alone and spoke as though it was just something he wanted to do. Had it been a money raising venture then he'd have had at least one mate with him to back him up and look after his welfare. What's more, he wouldn't stop somewhere for six days. He'd want to move on."

"Yes, that's true, I suppose," conceded Kate.

"So we have two options to look into," stated Ivy. "One: it was robbery and two: it was to shut him up on the off chance he knew what happened to Harold."

"I agree," said Dilly.

Everyone else nodded.

"I wonder when the post mortem will be," mused Amelia, "I mean, that might help. Not that we're likely to hear much about it."

"Ah, now I do know the answer to that," said Dotty. "Gerry mentioned it would be today."

As she spoke the door of the pub opened and in walked Gerry.

"Well, talk of the devil." Ernie beckoned him over.

After buying a drink, Gerry grabbed a spare chair from another table and sat down.

"Any news?" Amelia eagerly asked.

"There are a couple of things I can tell you. One, as expected, is that the cause of death was the blow to the back of his head. The second is a bit of a mystery. Apparently someone had stuffed an old lottery ticket inside the victim's mouth. And before you ask, we've no idea why, or if it's of any significance."

"A lottery ticket," gasped Dilly, "you're pulling our legs."

"I'm not. Really, I'm not, and again before you ask it was bought last Saturday and the numbers weren't winners."

Robin opened his mouth to speak and then closed it again; his eyebrows furrowed. Dotty noticed. "Are you alright, Robin? It's just you look puzzled."

"Yes, yes, I'm fine. It's just I'm trying to think about something an ex work colleague told me a while back. About a lottery ticket, that is."

"Does that mean the police were involved with whatever you're trying to recall?" Ivy was intrigued.

Robin nodded. "Yes they were and it's gradually coming back." He took a sip of his beer. "It was Phil who told me and it must be three months or so ago now. Phil of course being my old work mate. Anyway, someone, I can't remember his name and probably never even knew it, went to the police to report a stolen lottery ticket. Well, not so much stolen. You see, the person in question bought a ticket as he did every Wednesday and Saturday with just the one line with the same numbers every time, but because he was going on holiday he left the ticket with one of his flat mates. When he came back from his holiday he found the chap he'd left the ticket with had moved out. He was told this by the other two blokes he shared with who had no idea where he'd gone. Anyway, he thought nothing of it, then one day he decided to look back at old winning numbers and found the ticket he'd left behind would have won somewhere in the region of fifty thousand pounds. The police contacted Camelot and the money had been paid out to a Matthew something or other and there was nothing more anyone could do. The ticket was genuine and bought for cash so there was no way of proving who had purchased it. Furthermore, the cops felt the blokes in the flat were a bit dodgy and it was likely that the one who'd reported it was just trying it on. The case, such as it was, was then dropped."

"And the bloke the money was paid out to was called Matthew something or other. My goodness. Might it have been Polkinghorne?" Dilly asked.

"Possibly. I can't remember."

"Then you must ring this Phil and find out." Dotty picked Robin's phone up from the table and thrust it in his hand.

"Yes, yes, I will." Robin stood up and took his phone outside where it was quieter. When he returned his head was shaking. "Sorry to disappoint you all but his name wasn't Polkinghorne, it was Greyson. Phil remembers because his girlfriend's surname is Greyson too, but no relation of course."

"Damn!" Dotty cursed.

Ernie absent-mindedly tapped a beer mat against the table's surface. "It's just a thought, but if I were this Matthew bloke and I'd fiddled a mate out of fifty grand then I'd want to be untraceable. So perhaps the coastal path walk is just to keep him on the move. Meanwhile, to hide his true identity he changes his name every time he stops and books accommodation into whatever and wherever."

Dilly slapped her hands together. "I like it, Ernie. And it's possible when he arrived here he opted for the name Polkinghorne on impulse after spotting the plaque mentioning the late Henry's donation to create the sports room."

"Good theory," agreed Orville, "the plaque's clearly visible when standing at the bar so it's more than feasible."

"No, I don't buy that, because if he changed his name everywhere he went, he'd not leave coming up with a name until he was actually booking a room."

"You have a good point there, Ivy," acknowledged Dotty. "Does anyone know if he paid for things with a card or cash? Because if it was by card then it would have his name on it."

"Good thinking," Gerry stood up, "I'll ask Robert."

In less than a minute Gerry returned and sat back down. "He paid for everything with cash."

"Hmm, so what does that tell us?" Amelia tutted. "I mean, if his name really *was* Polkinghorne, it'd mean he wasn't the bloke who cleared off with the fifty grand. So how would that explain the lottery ticket?"

"Goodness only knows, and once again it seems we've hit a brick wall. And with this Matt chap being dead we can't ask him if Polkinghorne is his real name. Just as I expect George from way back is long dead too." Dotty tipped the last of her tonic water into her gin.

"So what's our next move?" Orville asked.

All shook their heads.

Kate suddenly sat up straight. "Oh my goodness," she gasped. "I've just realised there's a George at the care home.

He's one hundred and two years old so would have been around twenty when Harold was killed. Might he be our George Polkinghorne?"

"I doubt it. I mean, there's nothing to indicate that care home George lived here in the village," reasoned Larry.

"How can we find out?" Dotty asked.

Dilly was puzzled. "Are you talking about Mabel's boyfriend, Kate?"

"Yes, of course."

"But how do you know he's called George? Elsie always referred to him as Mabel's boyfriend."

Kate smiled. "Jenny Carne mentioned it. You see because Elsie Mitchell used to live at our place, Larry and I decided that now it's been done up we'd invite her out for a visit. When I asked her she was thrilled to bits and asked if Mabel and her boyfriend could come as well. I said of course. She then said I'd need to speak to either Jenny or Terry Carne about them leaving the care home and when I did Jenny jotted down the names, Elsie, Mabel and George."

"And he's one hundred and two," gasped Ivy.

"Exactly," confirmed Kate, "so there's a slim chance he could be our George Polkinghorne. Although I have to admit George was a very popular name back then. Anyway, because they'll be coming to our place next Tuesday, why don't we make a little party of it?"

"Are you asking us to be there as well?" said Ernie.

"Yes, the more of us there are then the more we're likely we are to find out if care home George is a Polkinghorne. And even if he isn't it'll be a bit of fun and we'll treat it as a house warming party."

"That's an excellent idea, Kate," acknowledged Dilly, with glee, "and to make it easier for you, we'll all do the usual and bring a plate of something or other."

"And a few bottles of booze too," added Ernie.

Chapter Twenty-One

On Monday morning, Dotty called at Lavender Cottage where she found Dilly alone.

"Come in, come in. I've been reading ever since breakfast so it'll be nice to give my poor old eyes a break. Tea or coffee?"

"Coffee please." Dotty sat down as Dilly took two mugs from the kitchen cabinet, spooned in coffee granules and reached for the kettle simmering on the Truburn.

"I've a pizza in the freezer that I keep meaning to use but it's really too big for one so if I pop it in the oven now would you like to share it with me?"

"That would be smashing, thank you. I didn't realise it was quite this late but that would explain why my tummy's rumbling."

Dilly switched on the oven to warm it up, fetched the pizza from the freezer and then poured water onto the coffee granules. "So what brings you here on this bright sunny morning? More gossip? It must be something like that because we'll all see each other tomorrow afternoon at Holly Cottage."

"You know me too well and yes the reason I'm here is because I thought you'd be interested to know that the police have arrested a man for the murder of Matthew Polkinghorne."

"They have? Already?" Dilly then frowned. "So after all our speculation it turns out his name really is Polkinghorne."

"Well no actually it's not. It's Matthew Greyson but I said Polkinghorne so you'd know who I meant."

"I see," Dilly stirred the coffee slowly as she digested information received, "so if he's Matthew Greyson, he must be the one who ran off with the winning lottery ticket."

"Yes, that's right. He is."

"I think I understand." Dilly handed Dotty her mug of coffee. "So who's been arrested? My fertile brain tells me it must be the chap Robin told us about. The one who had the fifty grand lottery money nicked. Is that right?"

"Spot on. Apparently the bloke who bought the winning ticket is called Wayne Hickson, and as you clearly remember Robin's old work colleague, Phil, said the bloke who'd run off with Wayne's fifty grand was called Matthew Greyson. So after Robin's call to Phil, Phil told a senior officer about our graveyard murder and he, the senior officer, contacted the Force down here to see if there might be a connection. The police here agreed that because of the lottery ticket in Matthew's mouth, there most likely was. So the police up-country looked back for details of the theft reported by Wayne Hickson and sent a couple of officers round to his address to question him. And guess what? He wasn't in, but his flatmates said he'd gone off to Cornwall. Anyway, the police up there told the police down here who put out a search and picked him up last night."

After checking the oven was hot enough, Dilly placed the pizza on the top shelf. "And has he confessed?"

"Yes, which is just as well because there's plenty of evidence against him anyway. Fingerprints for example. Matthew was hit with a heavy vase taken from one of the graves which the police found discarded in the long grass. There are prints on it and it's assumed there will be a match. There's also CCTV footage of Wayne buying diesel at a garage in St Austell and he's wearing clothing identical to that as described by a witness who'd seen a man lurking in the graveyard on the evening Matthew was killed."

Dilly slowly shook her head. "So by pushing an old lottery ticket in Matthew's mouth, the murderer rather gave himself away. What a Muppet."

"Yes, that's just what Gerry said. But then in all fairness had Robin not made the connection the case might never have been solved. As it is, it's probably the quickest murder case solved ever."

"Well, I'm glad it's sorted but I wonder how this bloke Wayne Hickson, knew where to find Matthew Greyson."

Dotty took a sip of coffee. "I was about to get onto that because really that's the interesting bit and believe it or not, it actually does relate to Harold Jenkins."

"Really?" Dilly jumped up and grabbed her mobile phone from the sideboard. "I won't give you more than one guess as to whom I'm ringing."

Amelia arrived promptly carrying a half-eaten sandwich on a plate. Apologising for bringing her lunch, she sat down.

"So," said Dilly, as she made coffee for Amelia, "what's the connection, Dotty?"

"Well, a few months ago, our now deceased Matt was in a pub near to his home. This was before he did a runner with the lottery ticket and I'll call him Matt because it's easier than keep saying Matthew Greyson. Anyway, Matt was in a pub and a bloke who'd had one too many was holding forth about a distant female relative who might have bumped someone off. This raised Matt's curiosity so he joined the group of people already listening to learn the details. I don't know the Christian name of the inebriated bloke but he claimed that his Great Uncle Percy used to live in St Austell and was the cousin of the female who'd bumped the 'someone' off. And this is the interesting bit. She, the female in question, was called Betty. Betty Reynolds would you believe!"

"No surely not," Dilly jumped up when the oven pinged to say the pizza was ready.

“Yes, she was, and not only that but it turns out that the drunken bloke was a Reynolds too.”

“So why did this drunken Reynolds chap think Betty was a murderer?” Dilly removed the pizza from the oven and placed it on the ceramic hob.

“Well it appears that during this Reynolds bloke’s ramblings, he claimed that according to his Great Uncle Percy, a male friend of Betty had disappeared into thin air back during the war. And because she, Betty, did a runner after he was found to be missing, it was reckoned by some family members that she knew exactly what had happened to him. The great uncle, long dead of course, had claimed his cousin Betty was never the same after the bloke disappeared and looked as guilty as sin. When one of the blokes in the pub asked where this had all happened, he said at some God-forsaken place in Cornwall called Trenwalloe Sands…”

“…God-forsaken,” gasped Dilly, “cheeky so-and-so.”

“That’s just what I said.”

“So what happened next and how do you know this, Dotty?” Amelia having finished her sandwich placed the plate on the floor by her feet and picked up her mug of coffee.

“I know because Gerry told me. What I’m telling you was part of Wayne Hickson’s confession.”

“Wayne being the chap who killed Matt in the churchyard,” Dilly wanted to make sure she had her facts right.

“Correct.”

“But how did this Wayne know Matt would be down here?” Amelia was puzzled.

“Quite simple really. You see, when Matt got home from the pub to the flat he shared on the night he’d heard the accusations against Betty Reynolds, Wayne was still up. So Matt told Wayne about the drunk and said that he’d a good mind to go down to Cornwall and look for anyone named

Reynolds on the off-chance they'd be related to the infamous Betty Reynolds. And if he found them, he'd demand they paid him to keep his mouth shut. At the time Wayne thought it was the beer talking, but after Matt ran off with his fifty grand winning ticket, it dawned on him that Matt really was dishonest. Wayne then wondered if Matt might have come down here looking for anyone named Reynolds in order to blackmail them as he'd said he might, but he dismissed the idea as unlikely. Then last week he saw on social media that a body had been found in a Cornish cellar at a place called Trenwalloe Sands. The name clicked and he then knew he'd been on the right track. So came down to find him and get his money back."

"This is making my head hurt," groaned Amelia.

"Mine too," Dilly stood and sliced the pizza having given it a few minutes to cool, "so it looks like Matt was the one who sent the blackmail letter to Libby and Luke. And if so it might explain why he was in the graveyard. I'm thinking along the lines of him trying to find out who previous members of the Reynolds family were to give him ammunition for further accusations."

"You're right, Matt was the blackmailer. Gerry said they found a notepad in his room at the pub with the indentation of what he'd written to Luke and Libby on the page beneath one that had been torn out. If you see what I mean."

Dilly handed three slices of pizza to Dotty. "So let me get this straight. Matt Greyson who called himself Matt Polkinghorne, some time ago met a drunken man in a pub who claimed he was a distant relative of Betty Reynolds, through his Great Uncle Percy, who had been Betty's cousin. And now Matt is dead, killed by this Wayne bloke, who Matt had fiddled out of a fifty grand lottery win."

"Correct."

"I don't believe it. What rotten luck. To think someone who knew something about Harold's death was right here on our doorstep and we didn't even see him, let alone get a chance to speak to him."

"True, but there's no way we'd have got anything out of him even if we had met him," reasoned Amelia. "He was down here to blackmail for money so would never have let on what he knew."

"No, I suppose not. And for all we've just learned about Matt's presence in the village and his death, it helps us not one jot to find out what happened to poor Harold."

"Oh but it does," said Dotty, "at least it might. Remember, it's because Matt used the name Polkinghorne that we've latched onto that name, and it's why we're partying at Holly Cottage tomorrow."

"You're right. So let's hope that care home George is indeed George Polkinghorne."

Chapter Twenty-Two

Tuesday dawned a beautiful day; 'wall to wall' sunshine, crystal clear visibility and not a cloud in the cornflower blue sky. Kate cleaned the windows and spent the morning making sure the house looked its best while Larry cut the grass, deadheaded the roses and swept a few fallen leaves from the newly laid patio outside the French doors. As Kate washed down the front door, Becky arrived to collect Mike and Jamie. Their plan for the day was to scour the churchyard again for any names they may have missed on their previous visit that might relate to Harold's case. They knew the vicar intended at some point to look through the church records for the names the headmistress had uncovered but conceded he might be otherwise engaged. For over the next few days in a nearby village where he also presided he was due to officiate at two weddings, a funeral and a baptism, hence might not have much spare time.

"So who's this party for?" Mike asked, as he slipped on his trainers. "Jamie said something about the old lady who used to live here. I know you go to visit her, but what's her name?"

Kate wrung out the wet cloth and rubbed over the clean door. "She's called Elsie Mitchell and with her will be two of her friends. Mabel Bennett who is one hundred years old and Mabel's boyfriend, George, who is one hundred and two. We don't know George's surname but we're hoping it might be Polkinghorne."

Mike's jaw dropped. "One hundred, and one hundred and two. Wow! Can we meet them?"

"Of course and I'm sure they'd love to meet you too. They'll be here by three so come back any time after that then the food will be ready and everyone should be settled and feeling at home."

Just after two, Dilly arrived at Holly Cottage along with Orville and Ivy; each carrying bags of delicacies and bottles of wine. After Kate left to pick up the guests of honour at the prearranged time of half past two, Larry showed Dilly, Ivy and Orville around the garden to view the recently created pond and see the new sandstone patio. They then returned indoors and helped Larry lay out the food and drink ready for the arrival of everyone else.

When Kate stepped into the care home she found Elsie, Mabel and George, all ready and waiting in the foyer; the ladies were wearing summer dresses and sunhats and George, lightweight beige trousers and a short sleeved shirt. With a little help from one of the carers the three were soon settled inside Kate's car where they chattered away like excited school children.

"This is just so wonderful," gabbled Mabel, from the back seat. "I can't remember the last time I had a trip out."

"Same goes for me," agreed Elsie, "and I'm longing to see my old house again, especially the roses."

Kate glanced in the rear view mirror at their happy faces and smiled. "That's good to hear, ladies, and to make this afternoon even more special, Larry and I have invited some of our friends along to join us as they're longing to meet you all."

"Will Dilly and Amelia be there?" Elsie who had already met the ladies in question asked.

"Yes, and so will Amelia's husband, Ernie, and Orville, Dilly's umm, well, to make it easy let's call him her fiancé even though strictly speaking he's not. Plus several others of course but not too many as to overwhelm you."

Mabel rubbed her hands together. "How exciting. I do love a party and I love meeting people too."

As Kate started the engine, George turned to face the ladies in the back of the car. "If you've mentioned it before, Elsie, I must have forgotten. Where you used to live, that is. I know you refer to home as the village but I've no idea of its name."

"Trenwalloe Sands," said Elsie, with pride, "it's a village by the sea and is quite big, but still the sort of place where everyone knows everyone else."

"Oh, never heard of it. At least I don't think I have. Oh, I don't know. It's so easy to forget things these days."

Mabel looked thoughtful. "The name seems to ring a bell with me but then there are a lot of places in Cornwall and when you get to my age you've forgotten more than you remember."

"Don't I know it," chuckled Elsie.

George agreed. "I was familiar with all the stately homes and their gardens in this country once upon a time but I'd be hard pressed to name half a dozen now."

When the car pulled up alongside the grass verge, Elsie squealed with delight. "Oh, it looks just as I remember it and you've kept the door white. I'm so glad. Tom and me both agreed white's the best colour for a door because it doesn't clash with anything."

Kate was glad she had washed it.

"But is white actually a colour?" George teased.

"Oh, stop it, George. You know what I mean."

No sooner had Kate switched off the engine than Elsie had the car door open and like a child on Christmas morning she had stepped out onto the grass verge and was clapping her hands with glee. Mabel, who was a little less agile, waited for Dilly who had been standing by the gate to give her a hand.

On hearing voices, Larry appeared in the front doorway to welcome the small party but before shaking hands, Elsie stopped to take in the fragrance of the roses.

"I think this has to be one of the happiest days of my life," she laughed, "It's just wonderful to take a trip down memory lane." She then took Larry's hand and clasped it warmly, "And you must be Kate's husband."

"I am indeed and Larry's the name."

"Lovely name. I had a brother called Larry. He was such a joy to us and our children adored him but sadly he died shortly before his fiftieth birthday."

"Oh, I am sorry to hear that," Larry escorted Elsie across the threshold, "So how many children do you have?"

"Just the two, both girls and both married. Marilyn is fifty-nine and lives in Yorkshire, and Susan, who's fifty-seven, lives in Cardiff. They visit me when they can but I don't want to be a burden and insist they put their own families first."

As the party made their way indoors, Kate returned to her car to help George get out. Gratefully, he took her arm. "What a glorious view," he pointed his walking stick to the surrounding countryside. "And the garden, what a lovely size."

"Yes, it is and I'm longing to dig up parts of the lawn to make more flower beds. The area out the back is a good size too and we have a stream running through the far end. We've widened part of it and created a little pond."

"You must show me before we go then because I'm a sucker for water features. I used to be a gardener, you know. A long time ago of course. I worked on National Trust and private estates in Devon and Cornwall over the years and loved every minute of it."

"Well, as you're on your feet I'll show you now. A friend kindly gave us some aquatic plants and they're already looking pretty good." Kate told Larry what they proposed to do and then escorted George along the hallway and out of the back door.

As they left, Larry turned to Mabel, who was still clutching Dilly's arm. "And you must be Mabel. I've heard what a marvel you are and you certainly don't look your one hundred years."

"You old flatterer you," she chuckled, as she lowered herself down beside Elsie, "I don't feel my age either but I'm not the oldest here, you know. George is two years older than me." She looked around. "Where is he?"

"My wife's taken him to see the stream in the back garden."

"Oh, not surprised. He loves his gardens does George and he's often asked for advice by our gardener at the care home," Mabel plumped up the cushion by her elbow. "What a lovely big room. So bright and airy."

"It is," agreed Elsie, "When we were here though this room was one of two but I much prefer it like this and I love the fact the back window has been replaced by patio doors."

Dilly pulled up a dining chair beside the couch. "Elsie told us that you used to live in Mevagissey, Mabel, and that you were married to a fisherman. Sounds very romantic."

Mabel laughed, "Well, yes. Not quite sure how to answer that. I mean there was a lot of anguish when my Tom was at sea, especially during bad weather and the stuff he wore was a devil to wash by hand before I had my twin tub. Fish scales used to stick to everything, you see, so I had to soak the clothes before I washed them. Not an enviable job I can assure you and certainly not romantic."

Dilly pulled a face. "Ugh, no, sounds most unpleasant."

"So did you always live in Mevagissey?" Larry asked.

"No, I was living in St Austell when I met my husband and we were married there. But then as you know, St Austell's only a stone's throw from Mevagissey. Well, six miles thereabouts."

As Kate returned from the back garden with George there was a knock on the open front door. Amelia and Ernie stood on the doorstep, Ernie clutching bottles of wine and Amelia holding a Victoria sandwich freshly made that morning.

"Sorry we're later than expected," said Amelia, her face flushed, "my hair appointment took longer than I'd anticipated because one of the girls was off sick."

Kate smiled sweetly as she helped George into an armchair, "Well it looks lovely, Amelia, so was well worth the delay."

As George made himself comfortable, Larry welcomed the latest arrivals. "All here now, so shall we have a drink?" He placed Ernie's bottles of wine on the sideboard and Kate took the cake into the kitchen where she returned with it sliced and set it in the centre of the dining table along with other buffet food.

"We're not quite all here," said Dilly, "Freddie and Max, and Dotty, Gerry and Robin have yet to arrive, but then Dotty said they'd probably be a bit late. Freddie and Max likewise, so yes it's fine to start without them."

"It's like Christmas," said Mabel, as Larry handed her a schooner of sherry. Elsie opted for a glass of Ernie's elderberry wine.

Meanwhile, Ernie, seeing the ideal opportunity to establish George's surname, turned to the elderly gentleman. "Are you a wine man or would you prefer beer, Mr er…um…err?"

"…Oh please call me George and I'd like to try a drop of that elderberry wine of yours. It's a lovely colour."

Noting Ernie's unsuccessful attempt caused Dilly to smile; to reverse the look of disappointment on his face she decided to be blunt. As Ernie poured George a glass of elderberry wine, she asked, "George, is your surname by any chance Polkinghorne?"

George looked surprised. "Polkinghorne? Polkinghorne? No, no, it's Hicks. Yes, it's Hicks and always has been."

"Hicks! Oh," Dilly's voice rang with dismay.

"Polkinghorne," repeated Mabel, "You're not George Polkinghorne."

"I know, love. That's what I just said to the good lady."

The good lady tutted and whispered to Amelia by her side, "Oh dear. It's back to the drawing board then."

Freddie arrived with Max, and Dotty with Gerry and Robin shortly after the first arrivals began to eat. After introductions were made and all had devoured as much as they were comfortable with, Kate suggested they take their drinks outside and sit in the front garden to enjoy the warm afternoon sun. All agreed, especially Elsie who was keen to smell her roses again. While the garden furniture was taken by the older members of the group, the younger guests were happy to sit on cushions and blankets spread out on the grass.

Half an hour later as they sat outside and George, having enjoyed two glasses of Ernie's elderberry wine, slept soundly on one of the plush garden chairs, Jamie, Mike and Becky arrived back having taken longer than expected. For having found no gravestones for the names linked to Harold, Jamie, who still believed the apple tree had been trying to tell them something, insisted they look at all gravestones from the end of the twentieth century to the present day for names such as Isaac, Newton or Bramley, in fact anything that might be connected to apples. However they were out of luck and Mike declared the mission 'fruitless', a comment that received a withering look from Jamie and a chuckle from Becky.

Looking forward to something to eat and an ice cold drink, Jamie opened the gate and they all stepped onto the garden path. Most of the guests knew the three young people but when Mabel saw them her eyes became transfixed on Mike; her jaw slowly dropped and to the surprise of all, her frail hands flew to her face. "Arthur," she muttered, "Oh, my God. Arthur. Where did you come from?" Her hands shook and her lips quivered as Mike thinking there must be someone behind him, looked over his shoulder to see who she was staring at. Seeing no-one there, he looked at Larry and Kate hoping they might explain.

"No, Mabel," said Kate, kindly, "This young man isn't called Arthur, he's my grandson's friend and his name is Mike."

Mike nodded vigorously. "That's right."

Mabel shook her head, "No, no, I'd recognise that face anywhere. Arthur, tall, dark and handsome. We were at school together, you know, and now he's back and would you believe it, he's wearing my necklace."

Kate knelt down on the grass and gently stroked Mabel's arm. "No Mabel, it can't be your necklace. Perhaps you have one like it."

Confused, Mabel placed her hand by her throat. "No, it's my necklace. Where did you find it, Arthur?"

"Mike found it in a cave, Mabel." Kate was concerned by the change in Mabel's voice and the worried look on Mike's face.

"And I'm not Arthur. I'm Mike and this M is for Mike." Mike was aware they'd considered the M was possibly for Maggie but definitely not Mabel.

Seeing his friend was shaking, Jamie dashed into the house and returned minutes later with Mike's wallet. From it he took a rowing club membership card and showed it to Mabel. "See from the photo and name on this card. It says he's Mike, my Mike, Michael Rigg and I've known him since we were at pre-school together."

Momentarily it seemed Jamie's words had calmed Mabel, "Oh, silly me. Silly, silly me, but you look just like Arthur." She then looked around and caught sight of the house name engraved on the open gate and her face changed again. "Holly Cottage," she whispered, "Oh no, I've been here before, haven't I?" She stood up. "I recognise the lane now." Clutching her throat she looked towards the front door. "No," she whispered, "It can't be. Please no, it can't be." Grabbing her walking stick she made her way towards the house. All followed except George who was still asleep and having turned his head was snoring quietly. As Mabel entered the house and strode down the hallway she looked at the back door, raised her arm, opened it and stepped outside. With a trancelike expression on her face she ran her eyes over the back of the house, her face devoid of colour. She then returned indoors, stumbled back down the hallway and turned right into the kitchen where she paused momentarily, her eyes fixed on the gleaming kitchen floor tiles. With small, steady steps she then crossed the floor towards the slightly open door of the cupboard beneath the stairs. Slowly she pulled it open and peeped inside. When her eyes focussed on the trapdoor, she screamed. "No, no, no. You must have found him. You must have found Harold."

Chapter Twenty-Three

Nearest to the understairs cupboard, Larry and Kate leapt forward and each grabbed one of Mabel's arms as she tottered backwards, her whole body trembling as she attempted to stifle sobs. They then escorted her into the sitting room and lowered her down onto the couch. No-one dared speak as Mabel stared at the floor. Suddenly she looked up; her eyes searching the room until she spotted Mike. "I'll have to tell them, won't I, Arthur? I'll have to explain. I mean it's only fair even though it was such a long time ago."

Mike, suddenly, looking older than his thirteen years, nodded his head and then sat by her side. "Yes, yes, it might be for the best." His frightened eyes darted from face to face, looking for approval. Hoping he'd said the right thing.

Kate nodded. "Yes, Mabel. Mi…M…Arthur's right. You need to tell us what happened to Harold. That's if you can remember after all this time." In a daze, she knelt down on the floor, muddled thoughts flashing through her mind. Where did Mabel fit in? They thought there was a slim chance George might be linked to Harold if he were a Polkinghorne, but not Mabel.

The centenarian stopped trembling. The tone of her voice changed. "Oh I remember. It's still there. It's always been there but over the years I've pushed it right to the back of my mind and tried to forget. But now. Today. It's all coming back as fresh as a daisy."

Elsie sat, a look of confusion on her face, trying to make sense of the on-going conversation. Questions buzzed around in her head. Who was Harold? She had lived in the house for sixty years so where did the trapdoor in the cupboard come from? Why did Mabel insist the poor lad called Mike was someone she'd known at school called Arthur? Elsie wanted to ask but at the same time was too baffled to speak.

Mike meanwhile, took Mabel's hand in his and smiled at her. She smiled back and then looked at the eager faces watching her. "Betty, Betty Reynolds, was one of my dearest friends and she lived just down the road from here. Her parents both worked at the Manor. Her dad was a gardener and her mum was the cook."

"And Betty and her parents lived at Willow Cottage," Kate recalled the vicar telling of her baptism.

"Yes, that's what it was called. Willow Cottage. Fancy you knowing that. I'd not have remembered had you not said. It was a nice place and had a pretty garden but then I suppose Betty's dad had green fingers. Him being a gardener. And during the war he worked in one of the farms where he was in charge of growing crops. Anyway, Betty, me and the others all went to the school here in the village and so we had known each other for years." She paused and smiled at Mike, "We were good friends, all of us and then when we were in our late teens the war broke out and the lads had to go away. A year or so later, Betty, Sarah and me, Sarah being Sarah Cooper, left our jobs and went to work at a munitions factory. It was when the lads were both home on leave that it happened. Happy to be together again and eager to make use of the precious time, we used to meet up after work, go to the beach; go for walks and sometimes just sit and chat. As I've already said, we were all friends and had been for years. On Sunday, September 12th after we'd been for a walk, Harold said he fancied a drop of rum but he didn't want to go to the pub because being wartime there was little choice other than beer and also his parents ran the place, so it'd be like being at home for him." Mabel chuckled, "He probably didn't want anyone to see his black eye either. He told us he did it when he walked into a door. We all placated him of course but guessed the real reason was he'd taken a tumble while under the influence.

Liked a drink did Harold. But whatever, he convinced us that another reason he didn't want to go to the pub was because he was reluctant to talk about the war, a subject some of the old timers from the Great War seemed keen to discuss. Perhaps talking about it helped them, but Harold knew there were limits as to what they could say anyway. So with the pub being out of bounds, Betty suggested Archie's marrow rum. He used to make it, you see, and it was very, very popular amongst the men folk."

Ernie's eyes shone at the mention of marrow rum. A homemade beverage he'd read about but never made.

"Would that be Archie Penrose who lived here?" Larry wanted to make sure he had the facts right. "The Archie who made the rum, I mean."

"Yes, that's the chap. He lived here with his wife Mavis and their two children. Then when war was declared he promptly signed up and Mavis went off up-country with the children to look after her mother, leaving the house empty. Anyway, Sarah was not at all happy about Betty's suggestion and said in no uncertain terms that to pinch Archie's rum would be dishonest. But Harold liked the idea and reminded us all that by then poor Archie was dead. Killed in 1942, so he'd never come back. He also told Sarah that if it made her feel better, we'd tell Mavis, if she came home, that we'd pinched a bottle and we'd be happy to pay for it. But deep down we didn't think she'd care because she didn't like it anyway. She was very religious, you see, was Mavis, and anti-drink too. What's more, rumour had it that the Manor House and cottages were likely to be sold after the war and even if they weren't, Mavis might not be entitled to live here because it was Archie who worked for the manor."

"But surely the people who owned the manor wouldn't have turfed her out," spluttered Ivy. "I mean, her husband fought for King and country and it wasn't her fault that he had been killed."

"I'd like to think you're right and you probably are but we thought her returning unlikely anyway. She wasn't a Cornish lass, you see, and I always got the impression she didn't really like it down here. Apart from Archie and the twins all her family were up-country, Newbury, I think, and she always hoped she'd be able to persuade Archie to up sticks so they could all go and live there. In the end fate stepped in and she got her wish but not in the way she'd wanted."

Mabel paused to catch her breath and seeing she looked a little flustered, Kate went into the kitchen to get her a glass of water.

"Thank you, love." She took several gulps, "Now where was I?"

"Thinking of pinching Archie's marrow rum." Jamie, mesmerised, was hanging on to every word.

"Yes, that's right, we were and we knew we wouldn't have to break in because it was common knowledge that the spare back door key was outside under a stone. So that's what we did. We got the key and let ourselves in the back door. Trouble is, we couldn't find the rum. We looked in the kitchen and the sideboard in the living room. We didn't think it'd be upstairs but we looked anyway, then went back to the kitchen and out into the washhouse, but there was no sign of it. As a last resort we looked in the cupboard under the stairs and that's when we saw the trapdoor to the cellar. Betty told us it might be down there because they had a cellar at her house and her mum used to store all sorts of stuff in it. I didn't like the idea of going below ground and offered to stay in the cupboard to listen out in case someone should turn up. Not that I really thought anyone would. It was Arthur here who opened up the trapdoor and we all peered inside but it was as black as pitch. Knowing we needed a light, Harold ran his hands round the walls looking for a switch. He found it between shelves but when he flicked it on, nothing happened. We assumed the electricity was switched off. Either that or there was no bulb or it'd blown. Not to be deterred we looked around for a torch and

Sarah found one in a drawer by the sink. Its bulb was quite dim but there was just about enough light to see by. Harold took the torch and said he'd go first." Mabel's voice croaked as she paused and blinked away tears, "On the first step he pulled back as his face brushed against a cobweb. Betty, who was behind him, laughed, called him a scaredy-cat and gave him a push. He lost his footing on the second step and grabbed the wooden handrail. But it gave way and he fell head first over the side and onto the solid floor where he hit his head on a dirty great vice. Arthur pushed Betty aside and ran down after him. Blood was gushing from a wound on the back of Harold's head. Betty, Sarah and me went down to try and help but there was nothing we could do. I held his hand as his heart stopped beating and he took his last breath." Mabel paused, clearly upset. Her voice little more than a whisper. "Can you imagine what it was like? We didn't know what to do. Betty was in a terrible state, but she stood up and said she'd go and get her dad, who as I said, lived next door." Mabel turned to look at Mike. She shook her head, "But you stopped her, didn't you, Arthur? You asked her to think of the consequences. We were trespassing, our intent to steal. Furthermore, we couldn't prove Harold had fallen. It could be said one of us had pushed him deliberately or even hit him over the head with something or other. And if we were accused of murder and were found guilty then we'd all hang."

As the penny dropped Elsie looked aghast. "So would I be right in thinking this all happened here. In my old house. In a cellar that I never even knew existed? In fact it didn't exist because it wasn't there when we lived here. The cupboard had a solid floor covered in lino, same as the kitchen. So what did you do with it and how come it's there now?"

Mabel nodded. "Yes, it all happened here and I'll explain about the cellar."

Elsie fanned her face with a placemat. "I can't believe it. To think I lived here all those years knowing nothing about it."

“I’m sorry.”

“How can you remember all that happened in such detail?” Despite the severity of Mabel’s revelations, Amelia was in awe.

Mabel smiled through her tears. “That’s the thing about getting old,” she tapped her head, “it’s all there stored away in the memory and when something triggers it off and gets in the right groove it all comes flooding back like it was yesterday. Daft really because if you asked me what I had for breakfast today I’d not have the foggiest idea.”

“So what did you do?” Dilly asked, eager to hear more, “After you’d decided you couldn’t tell anyone.”

“What? Oh yes, we all went up to the kitchen and then into the front room where we quickly went over our options. As I’ve already said, telling someone was out of the question so it seemed there was only one thing we could do. We had to leave him there. We convinced ourselves that the cellar would be like a crypt. No-one would disturb him and he’d be able to rest in peace. It sounds so callous now but back then when the adrenaline was pumping it seemed the sensible thing to do. Betty said we must wrap him in something and Sarah suggested a thin rug that lay on the kitchen floor. We all agreed and as Sarah rolled it up and carried it down the cellar steps, I took down a crucifix I’d noticed hanging above an old Cornish Range.”

“Cornish Range,” interrupted Kate, “so there was one in the fireplace back then. We thought as much.”

“Yes, I don’t know if Mavis used it though because it looked very careworn and there was an old electric stove over by the sink.”

Larry scowled. “Sorry about my wife interrupting your flow, Mabel. Please continue.”

Kate looked sheepish. “Yes, I’m sorry.”

“That’s okay, dear, but where was I?”

“You’d just taken the crucifix from the wall.” Larry thought of the calendar, beneath which the image of the cross had remained for eighty years despite efforts to cover it with paint.

"Yes, of course. So with the rug stretched out on the cellar floor we carefully laid Harold on it and I placed the cross between his hands. We then wrapped the rug around him and carried him into a corner. Arthur who had once been a choir boy, said a few prayers. We all sang 'Abide with me,' and then we left him there and closed the trapdoor, having decided to return the next day and seal the cellar up. When we went back outside, the light was beginning to fade and we knew we needed to get home quickly before blackout. I went back with Betty, picked up my bike from her place and then pedalled back home as quickly as I could. Arthur meanwhile went to the pub and crept in the back door while Harold's parents and his sister were working in the bar. From Harold's room he took a rucksack and filled it with some of his belongings. He then crept back downstairs and from the shed took Harold's bicycle and rode it to a nearby field where he left it beside a hedge overnight. Desperate to get indoors before it was completely dark, he ran home carrying the rucksack, but before he went inside he dropped it behind the shed at the bottom of the garden intending to deal with it the following day."

"And the next morning he went to the pub to call for Harold, telling his parents they planned to go fishing but knowing full well that he wasn't there," said Kate.

Mabel nodded. "Yes, but how do you know that?"

"We've spoken to Harold's niece. Daughter of his sister, Grace. Of course she never knew her uncle but recalls her mother telling of how he went missing."

Mabel groaned. "Poor Grace. I knew I'd never be able to look her in the eye after that night. Not that we were friends anyway. She was a few years younger than us, you see, and so had her own set of friends."

"So what happened next?" Larry asked.

"After leaving the pub, as you said, having been there on the pretence of going fishing, Arthur rode Harold's bicycle into St Austell and left it outside the railway station. As he went to catch the bus back home, he passed a greengrocer's shop and saw they had apple trees for sale outside on the pavement. So he bought one. When he got home there was no-one in. His dad was at work and his mother at a group meeting where they knitted socks for the troops. So he went outside and dug a huge hole at the bottom of the garden, dropped the rucksack inside and after part filling in with earth he planted the apple tree. When his mother came home she was thrilled to bits. She always wanted an apple tree, you see, and in particular a Bramley."

"A Bramley apple tree!" Becky gasped, as something clicked into place. "I don't believe it." She looked at Mabel. "Was Arthur's surname Nicholas?"

"Yes, that's right. Now you come to mention it, it was."

Becky groaned. "I think I know the answer, but where did he live?"

"Oh, it was in one of the council houses. They'd not been built long back then and if I remember correctly it was in Glebe Road. Did you know him, dear?"

"No," Becky lowered herself onto the arm of a chair. "No, I didn't know him but I know the house he lived in and that he took over the tenancy after his parents died. And then in the nineteen-eighties he bought it from the council and lived there 'til he died, sixteen years ago."

Mabel looked confused; all thoughts of Mike being Arthur momentarily forgotten. "How do you know that?"

"Because I live in Arthur's old house. After he died the house went to a cousin who put it up for sale and my parents bought it."

As Kate glanced at the table where sat the remains of an apple pie made from the fruit of the very tree, it suddenly occurred to her who Mabel might be. For surely, Mabel was a shortened form of Amabella.

Chapter Twenty-Four

Being a practical man, Larry having digested Mabel's words, had a burning question. "I can follow everything you've told us so far but I'm intrigued to know how you went about sealing up the cellar. I mean, where did you get the bricks, cement, sand and what have you. Tools as well for that matter?"

Mabel smiled at Mike sitting by her side. "Arthur's dad worked on the railway but in his spare time he did some building work, having learned the trade when he left school. That meant Arthur had access to sand, cement and tools and so he took what was needed while his dad was at work and hid everything in the old wash-house here." Mabel looked at Larry and then cast her hand towards the back of the house, "The bricks used were from a part-tumbled down wall out there in the back garden. Of course, not wanting the cellar left accessible in case someone came round, Arthur started the job early the following evening. And then as soon as we got home from work, Betty, Sarah and me kept watch by lurking in the lane. We saw no-one though except an old boy walking a dog. So he didn't suspect anything we started picking blackberries. When he stopped by the garden gate and looked at the house, our hearts sank. We thought he might have heard something, but then after a few seconds he carried on walking, much to our relief. Anyway, Arthur got the job done and the next night he went back in to finish it off. It was the last chance he had before returning to his ship the following day. To his relief the cement had dried, so he laid a spare bit of lino he found rolled up in the corner of the cupboard, over his handiwork.

He made a good job of it. It matched the kitchen floor and no-one would have been any the wiser. Except Mavis of course, but as I've already said, we thought it unlikely she'd come back unless it was to pick up a few things she'd left behind. And if she did that we hoped she wouldn't notice." Mabel hung her head, "As you can imagine, talk of Harold's disappearance was rife in the village over the next few days and someone even suggested he'd deserted and done a runner. We wanted to quash that idea but had to be careful. It hurt us greatly though hearing his name dragged through the mud."

Amelia tutted. "So why on earth did Arthur leave Harold's bike at the railway station then? I mean, surely by doing so you'd have realised it'd cause people to latch onto the idea of desertion."

"It never occurred to any of us that that's what people might think. We'd assumed they'd just think he'd taken off for a couple of days. You know, to make use of the last few hours of his leave. But I suppose in retrospect that was silly because had he gone away for a few days he'd have told his parents and his sister."

"And it didn't help the situation by Arthur pretending that he and Harold had planned to go fishing on the morning he was found to be missing," chided Ivy, "That was very silly, if I might be permitted to say so."

Several heads nodded in agreement with Ivy's reprimand.

"Did the police ever look into Harold's disappearance?" Larry knew Nora's take on the question but because she was only a child back then he wanted it confirmed.

"Yes and no. Jack Harvey, the local bobby, was informed but you have to remember there was a war on. He did question our parents though to see if our stories tallied. You know, what time did we get in the night before Harold was found to be missing. He questioned us too of course but we all told the same story. That being as the light started to fade we made our way to our respective homes. He seemed happy with what we told him and assumed Harold had gone off of his own accord. I think when he didn't report back after his leave, the Army were concerned though. They took a very dim view of desertion and if caught the deserters were likely to be imprisoned."

"Well, we know you're still here and have made one hundred but what happened to the others?" Dilly asked. "We know that Arthur remained in the village in what is now Becky's family home and that he died here, but what about Betty and Sarah."

"Yes, Arthur…" Mabel paused and looked at Mike. "You can't be Arthur, can you? Because as this young lady just said, he's dead. And if you were Arthur you'd be old now, like me."

Mike nodded his head. He looked relieved. "That's right, I'm not Arthur, I'm Mike."

"Oh dear, dear, silly me. Silly, silly me. But you look like him. Like I remember him when we were young." Mabel glanced at the eager faces waiting for more revelations. "Of course he's dead. He died in 2007. Arthur, I mean. I know that because I read it in the local paper. It mentioned his time served in the Royal Navy and his charity work. I only ever saw him once after Harold's death. I was walking round St Austell doing some shopping. He didn't see me because we were on opposite sides of the road. But even if he had seen me we'd have said nothing about that night. On that subject we'd all taken a vow of silence. But even from across the road I could see in his eyes that it haunted him. It haunted us all."

Thankful that Mabel had acknowledged he wasn't Arthur, Mike raised his hand. "Can I ask Mabel a question?"

Kate answered, "Of course, Mike, go ahead."

"Mabel, if you think this necklace is yours, when did you lose it?"

"Oh, I don't know. I always wore it day and night and never took it off. It was a birthday present from my grandmother who sadly died a few weeks after she'd given it to me. It was as I brushed my hair one morning, years ago, that I noticed it'd gone but I couldn't think where."

"Well, we found it in an old sack. It was caught on the inside of the shade of a table lamp along with a trumpet, a cricket bat, a prayer book, a picture and a cuckoo clock."

"And the sack was hidden deep inside a cave where no-one would have spotted it," Jamie added.

Mabel leaned her head back in the chair. "Oh dear, I know when I lost it then. You see, we all agreed that if Mavis came back to collect her stuff she'd notice her cross had gone from the wall and the kitchen rug was missing too. So we reasoned that we needed to make it look like the place had been burgled. I was given the job of gathering a few things together and stuffing them inside a sack, and Arthur said when I'd done it he'd put it somewhere it was unlikely ever to be found. The necklace must have fallen off when I was doing it. Well I never. Serves me right."

"It looks like this really is yours then, in which case you'd better have it back." Mike reached behind his neck to undo the clasp. Mabel took hold of his arm. "No, no, you keep it. At my time in life I don't need it anymore and I'd have a job to manage the clasp anyway now my eyes are not so good. But when you look at it think of me. Of us. All of us. And let it be a reminder to always be good and kind and thoughtful. Unlike we were."

Kate was confused. If the necklace belonged to Mabel then she couldn't be Amabella because her grandmother would not have chosen the initial of her shortened name. Disappointed with her surmise, she nodded at Mike to indicate he should do as Mabel asked. She then turned to the elderly widow. "We know about the necklace now and you've told us what happened to Arthur, but what became of Sarah and Betty?"

"I don't know a great deal, but after that night Betty said she was going to join the Women's Voluntary Service. I assume she did but if so I've no idea where she was based or for how long she served. As for her parents, I believe they moved from Willow Cottage to a little house in the village after the war. I've no idea whether or not Betty ever lived with them again but I doubt it because she said after and the war was over, she hoped to start a new life and live and work as far away from Cornwall and its harrowing memories as she could possibly get. As for myself, I'd already left by then for the same reason and with no intention of ever returning. We didn't keep in touch so I don't know anything about her life after Trenwalloe Sands. I don't even know if she ever married but I do know that she didn't outlive her parents. I saw her mum out shopping when she bumped into a woman in St Austell back in 1977. Her mum didn't see me but then she wouldn't have recognised me anyway. I'd lost a lot of weight since then, you see, and my hair was styled differently. It was a different colour too – grey would you believe. I heard her telling the woman that her Betty had died. I remember the year because it was our late Queen's Silver Jubilee."

Kate sighed. "And Sarah Cooper. Any idea what became of her?"

"Again I don't really know what happened to Sarah other than she planned to leave and go up-country somewhere. At that time she had lodgings with the school's headmaster and his wife. The wife being a good friend of her mother's. Sarah's father died when she was eleven years old, you see, and five or six years later her mother remarried and went to live in Truro with her new husband, who was a widower with two children. The reason Sarah stayed in the village was because she had friends here and conditions would be cramped in the home of her new stepfather. She also didn't want to leave Arthur having been his girlfriend for several years. Sadly that came to an end though after the night Harold died. With a heavy heart she broke off their relationship as soon as the cellar was safely sealed up. In fact she said she didn't want to see any of us ever again because we'd always remind her of that dreadful night. We quite understood and bore no grudge. In fact we all felt the same. I didn't go far. Just Exeter, but I missed Cornwall and so moved back to St Austell where I met my husband and then after we married I moved into his place in Mevagissey. I've no idea if Sarah married but I heard on the grapevine she'd had a son but I don't know whether or not it's true."

"SC loves AN," whispered Kate, "So it must have been Sarah who wrote that on the wall."

"Yes, of course," gasped Amelia, "Sarah Cooper loves Arthur Nicholas."

Mabel frowned. "What do you mean by wrote on the wall? Which wall and where?"

"Here," said Kate, "we found it scribbled underneath several layers of wallpaper."

"Really! She must have done that while we were looking for the rum then." Mabel glanced around the room, "Is it still there?"

"No, because the wall's gone now. We found it when we knocked it down to make this into one big room."

"We do still have it, Kate. Well a piece of it anyway." Larry jumped up and fetched the lump of plaster from the landing window sill and on returning placed it in Mabel's hands.

"Oh dear, you naughty girl, Sarah. I hope Arthur didn't see this. He'd have called it vandalism."

"Are you alright, Robin?" Dotty thought he looked unwell, "You've gone awfully pale."

"Yes, yes, I'm fine, at least I think I am and thank you for asking. But it all makes sense now." Robin, having absorbed Mabel's information, sat down on the arm of a chair and looked her in the eye. "You're right, you know,

Mabel. Sarah did have a son. She also got married but that was several years after she'd given birth. She called her son Nicholas. He was born in 1944 and Sarah's husband, Frank, adopted him and gave him his surname. The son currently lives in Peterborough. He married in 1980 and also had a son. I know this because Nicholas is my father."

Several people gasped.

"What?" Gerry, confused, rested his hand on Robin's shoulder. "Are you saying that Sarah Cooper was your grandmother, Rob?"

"Yes, yes I am. And Arthur, Arthur Nicholas must have been my grandfather although I never knew him or even knew his name. It's so silly, I can see it all clearly now but believe me, the penny's only just this minute dropped."

Dilly waved her hand around the people gathered. "Could you explain, please, Robin, because I'm sure, like me, everyone here is completely confused?"

"Yes, sorry, of course. Well, I'll try. You see, I knew that my grandmother came from Cornwall because she often mentioned it. But I knew nothing of my grandfather other than the fact that my grandmother, Sarah, whose maiden name was Cooper, never told anyone who the father of my dad was. We knew it wasn't her husband, Frank Hood, because as I've already said, she married him several years after Dad was born and he, Frank Hood, adopted Dad. They then went on to have a daughter. Dad's half-sister, my Aunt Beattie who currently lives in Penzance. All the same I had reason to believe that he, my unidentified grandfather, also came from Cornwall and felt my grandmother, might have left the county to avoid telling him of her pregnancy. But having heard Mabel's story it seems more than likely that she didn't even realise her condition when she left. The silly thing is, that I thought while down here I might do a bit of research into the family as well as for my next book. I knew Sarah, my grandmother, came from somewhere around here because she often mentioned St Austell, and I thought it'd be a good way to spend my time while Gerry was working. Little did I know I'd get roped into a murder case and of course when I did all thoughts of tracing my grandparents vanished."

Dilly was confused. "Okay, but why do you think Sarah and Arthur are your grandparents? I mean they're hardly uncommon names."

"Because the names and the dates tally. As I said my grandmother was called Sarah Cooper. So when Dotty showed me her phone with the names of school children from back then, I realised on seeing Arthur and Sarah's names together that there might possibly be a link. And now Mabel has confirmed my suspicion by saying that Sarah and Arthur were an item, so to speak. Another thing is that everyone calls my dad Nick, but his full name is Nicholas Arthur Hood. Nicholas Arthur being the reverse of Arthur Nicholas. What's more, his date of birth is June 17th 1944."

Dilly slowly nodded her head. "I see, yes, and as you say the dates tally."

"Precisely. And another thing, when I went down to Penzance to see Aunt Beattie, I told her in great detail about Harold Jenkins going missing eighty years ago and how his remains had been found. I also mentioned one of his friends might have been my grandmother because according to school records, a Sarah Cooper, born in 1921, went to Trenwalloe Sands School, and 1921 is the year my grandmother was born. Aunt Beattie was very interested and said she remembered my grandmother, who was of course her mother, telling her about three of her friends from when she lived in Cornwall. Their names were Betty, Maggie and Amabella. That clicked instantly with me as I remembered those names were also on the school list."

"So Maggie must be Maggie Jones who disappeared," said Kate.

"That's the conclusion we came to but I didn't want to say anything until I was confident and as I said a few minutes ago, it's only just gelled with me that Arthur Nicholas must have been my grandfather."

"That's weird," said Kate, "but rather marvellous too."

"Was your aunt able to tell you anything about your grandmother's friends?" Amelia asked.

"Not a lot, but she recalls being told that Betty was self-assertive, Amabella was very clever and Maggie was a bundle of laughs."

Kate frowned. "Well we now know through you, Robin, what happened to Sarah, and we know Betty joined the Women's Voluntary Service, but I wonder what became of Maggie and Amabella." She turned and addressed their elderly guest, "Were they your friends too, Mabel?"

Mabel nodded. "Yes, and it's very sad. You see, Amabella who we called Bella, moved with her family to Plymouth in 1937. We missed her terribly after she'd gone and we all kept in touch. And then war broke out and in 1941 she and her entire family were all killed in an air raid. It still grieves me to think of it."

"Dreadful," whispered Kate, "I'm so sorry, Mabel."

"And Maggie?" Larry hardly dare ask, "What became of her?"

Mabel opened her mouth to speak but no words emerged.

Robin spoke on her behalf. "Aunt Beattie knew nothing about Maggie Jones going missing until I told her what Nora had said. You see, although Gran spoke of her friends in the days when they were young, she never mentioned the war or what happened to any of them or even why she herself left Cornwall. Having said that, you know very well what happened to Maggie Jones, don't you Mabel?" He rose from the arm of the chair and knelt down in front of the elderly lady, "I'm right, aren't I? You and only you know what happened to Maggie Jones."

Mabel gasped as her trembling hands flew to her mouth. "W…w…what do you mean?"

"I mean, I know who you are, Maggie. And I wonder, when did you change your name to Mabel?"

Mabel suddenly looked deflated; her shoulders slumped and her eyes filled with tears. "How did you work that one out?" she whispered.

"Just a minute, Robin. Are you saying that Mabel is the missing Maggie Jones?" Amelia looked flummoxed, "I…I don't understand."

Mabel gave a little cough to clear her throat. "And I don't expect you to. I don't expect any of you to. But believe me the pain was dreadful. It was too much. I knew Sarah planned to leave and I wanted to do the same but I couldn't face telling my parents because they'd try and stop me, so I had to run away. It was alright for Sarah. Her mother had remarried and was living in Truro so she was free to do as she pleased." She looked at Robin, "But I ask again, how did you know who I was?"

Robin took her two frail hands in his. "Because as well as Aunt Beattie telling me that Gran said Maggie was a bundle of laughs, she also said that the tip of the fore finger on her left hand was missing due to an accident at school when she trapped it in the hinge of the school gate. So I've put two and two together and it seems I've made four."

Mabel looked at her left hand held by Robin. "You have indeed, young man. You have indeed. Trust Sarah to remember that."

"I need a drink," Ernie poured himself a bumper glass of parsnip wine, the elderberry bottle being empty. Several others did likewise.

Amelia tutted. "Well, Mabel, if you're Maggie perhaps you can answer the question that confused everyone back then. That being, why on earth didn't you leave the note saying you were going on the table or somewhere like a normal person would have done, instead of pushing it through the letterbox so your parents would find it on the doormat."

"Quite simply because I forgot to leave it. That is to say, it was in my pocket because in one hand I had my suitcase and in the other a large bag. It was the middle of the night and it wasn't until I got outside that I remembered it and by then I'd shut the door. The door had a newly fitted Yale lock and I'd left my key in my room so I couldn't get back in. Posting it through the letterbox was my only option, but believe me I've kicked myself for that many times over the years."

"Your poor parents," murmured Kate.

"I know. I know and so often I wanted to go back and see them. To hug them and Patrick too. But I couldn't without saying why I'd left."

Dotty felt sorry for the elderly lady. "Don't upset yourself. What's done is done."

Amelia agreed. "Yes, you're right, Dotty, but what I'd like to know, is why you choose to call yourself Mabel Bennet?"

A tear trickled down Mabel's check. "My name is Mabel now because I changed it by deed poll. The reason for the choice is simple. When I was small I was a chubby little thing and Dad, dear, dear, Dad, used to call me Mabel after Mabel Lucie Attwell's illustrations of cuddly, rosy faced children. It was said with great affection. Bennet is my married name."

Chapter Twenty-Five

On Wednesday morning, Dilly, Kate, Amelia and Ivy went to see Nora. She had heard from her next door neighbour, Jill through Jill's son, Brett, that the mystery of Harold Jenkins had been solved at last, but all the same, she was pleased to see the ladies to hear their account of how the previous day had unfurled.

"So you were on the right track," said Nora, as she placed a plate of assorted biscuits on the table, "That being, you thought George thingy at the care home might be George Polkinghorne, but you just chose to pursue the wrong centenarian character."

"We certainly did," tutted Ivy, "and the daft thing is, while we were trying to track down any descendants of Harold's friends, there was one right there amongst us. Robin! Who's not just the descendant of one of the people involved, but the descendant of two."

"Oh dear. I hope he's alright," said Nora, "Poor lad. It must have come as a real shock."

"It did," said Dilly, "Having seen the name Sarah Cooper on the list of school pupils he thought the chance of her being his grandmother was more than possible, but what he didn't expect was any involvement in Harold's death. He was as white as a sheet when the reality of what happened back then struck him."

"He was," agreed Kate, "and then when he spotted Mabel's missing fingertip and realised who she was, everything made sense. Daft really, but it never occurred to any of us that Mabel could be Maggie Jones, although for a while I did wonder if she might have been Amabella."

"And Arthur," tutted Nora, "I remember him but we never called him that. He liked to be called Nick, probably because he wanted to feel he was a different person to who he was during the war. It never occurred to me he'd be a contemporary of Harold's and I suppose, unlike the others, he didn't leave the village because by the time the war was over and he was discharged from the Navy, time had healed some of the wounds. I vaguely remember him dying but he wasn't buried here. His will requested he be cremated and his ashes scattered in the garden of remembrance. All the same, not thinking of him – well, it was very remiss of me."

"Did you know him well?" Dilly asked.

"No, not at all. He'd have been a good ten years older than me. I knew him by sight but our paths never crossed and I believe he kept himself very much to himself. Almost hermit like."

Ivy nodded. "I remember as a child we were very wary of him. Mum used to feel sorry for him. Said he must have horrible memories of the war. Was probably even on a ship that went down. For that reason the war was not a subject to be broached in his presence. Now we know why he wanted to push memories of those days away."

"And it probably explains why he never set foot in the pub after the war either. People used to think it was odd that an ex-Navy man didn't drink but I suppose he associated alcohol and the pub with that dreadful night." Nora sighed. "Poor man. I mean were it not for Harold wanting a drink they would never have gone into the cellar or even the house in the first place. As it is that single unnecessary act caused the death of one and ruined the lives of four."

"It did," Amelia glanced at three courgettes on Nora's work surface, "and I should imagine the four who survived Harold would forever hate the sight of marrows, but at least it explains why Archie grew so many."

Kate chuckled to herself. "The boys are off home tomorrow and I'm really going to miss them. They've been a breath of fresh air this past fortnight and really threw themselves into trying to solve the mystery of Harold's death."

"They did a pretty good job too," agreed Amelia. "I mean finding the graves of the Cowlings and thinking the couple could be responsible for the SC loves AN scribblings was good, imaginative detective work, even if they were wrong."

"As a matter of interest, Nora, do you happen to know the maiden name of Annie Cowling?" Dilly asked, "It'd be a real coincidence if it began with the letter N."

"Annie Cowling. Now did her name begin with N? My goodness it was such a long time ago." Nora tapped her fingers rhythmically on the table top, "Yes, yes, you're right. Of course her maiden name began with N. She was a Newton before she married Sam. It's all coming back now. I remember the wedding, you see. It was just after the war ended and us girls, keen to see the bride, went along to watch them come out of the church. She was a real beauty and I remember she looked absolutely stunning in the very dress her mother had worn twenty years or so before when she got wed."

"Really!" Dilly gasped, "So the boys may have been right after all. But as it is, we'll never know for sure."

"It's only just occurred to me, but I wonder why Annie wasn't on Claudia's list of school children," mused Amelia, "If I remember correctly, it said on her gravestone that she was born in 1925, so a similar age to Grace Jenkins and Patrick Jones."

"Because she was home taught," said Nora, without hesitation. "Her mother, Nelly, was a school teacher who was injured when she fell off her bike and rolled down a hill badly hurting her back. It was thought she might never walk again but she did although with great difficulty and the pain meant she had to give up working. So to make it easier for everyone, when Annie became of school age,

Nelly taught her at home and Annie was able to help her mother around the house, thus enabling her dad to go to work. Then when war broke out, Nelly's sister, Beryl, lost her husband and because she couldn't afford to live on her own she moved in with the Newtons and took over looking after Nelly. This allowed Annie, who by then was in her teens, to find a job and work. Mum used to frequently tell me this story when I was young to make sure I always took great care when out on my bike."

"Poor lady, so out of curiosity, where did they live?" Kate asked.

"Somewhere along Back Lane. Annie's dad, Walter, was a farm worker and their home was one of the tied cottages owned by the Jones family. Walter, like Archie Penrose, played the trumpet in the band and they both played cricket too. I think I've already mentioned Archie was regarded as a talented batsman. Anyway, after they were married, Annie moved in with Sam at Cowlings Bakery along the main street. Sam being the baker, a job he'd done since leaving school. Cowlings Bakery was a family affair. It's long gone now though. Like so many things it was killed off by the supermarkets."

"Back Lane, so not too far from us then," said Kate, "We can see the lane just across the field from our back garden. Looks a nice spot with woodland in the background."

"Yes, and just the other side of the woods is Glebe Road where Arthur lived."

At Arthur's erstwhile home in Glebe Road, Becky, Jamie and Mike watched from a distance as the police dug around the base of the Bramley apple tree. As anticipated they eventually found tattered remnants of Harold's belongings deep beneath the tree, tangled with its twisted roots.

"To think," Mike grumbled in disgust, "we sat under that tree trying to fathom out what had gone on and all the while old Harold's things were just a few feet below us. Bonkers I call it."

"Ah, but the tree tried to tell us," said Jamie. "Remember the apple falling on my head? I said it was a sign and I was right. That tree was trying to tell us what was buried deep beneath its roots but you both poo-pooed it."

Becky laughed. "Well that's because you said we needed to look for a name linked to apples or Sir Isaac Newton which sent us on a wild goose chase round the churchyard."

On Wednesday afternoon, the police having found the buried belongings of Harold Jenkins, questioned Mabel Bennet and considered charging her with the offence of preventing the lawful and decent burial of a dead body. However, because of her age and her obvious remorse it was deemed she had suffered enough over the years; not just living with the guilt of what happened that September evening, but also with the loss of contact with her family and friends.

On Thursday morning, Kate collected Mabel, who insisted she still be known by that name, from the care home and drove her to the graveyard at Trenwalloe Sands.

In her hands the elderly lady clutched two bunches of flowers, a mixture of yellow chrysanthemums and purple Michaelmas daisies. One bunch she placed in the vase beneath the memorial stone erected by her brother Patrick in memory of his, their, parents. The other she placed in the granite memorial vase paid for by money raised in the village. For having no living relatives - so they thought - those who had known and liked Patrick thought it only fitting there should be something to indicate where his ashes lay.

After making enquiries on-line, Kate was able to tell Mabel that on his instruction, Patrick had left all his worldly goods including money from the sale of his house, to various charities. This pleased Mabel enormously and in a way helped lessen the burden she had carried for the past eighty years.

As they turned to leave, Mabel looked towards a large yew tree in a neglected part of the graveyard near to a bramble-covered boundary wall. "Kate, it won't take a moment but can we go over there, please?" She pointed her walking stick towards the tree.

Happy to oblige, Kate escorted Mabel along the path and then over the grass between rows of gravestones, monuments and memorials.

By the yew tree they stopped and Mabel pointed to a long forgotten grave with ivy part-covering its lopsided headstone. "Please read that for me. I can't remember the exact words now even though I knew it off by heart once upon a time."

Kate released her grip on Mabel's arm, pulled away strands of ivy and brushed aside the long grass. Behind it she read:

Here lies our dear son,
George Henry Polkinghorne.
Died April 18th 1937.
Aged 17
Taken from us far too young but now with the angels.
Rest in Peace.

As Kate stood up she saw Mabel brush away a tear.

"George and I were sweethearts and had been since we were at the village school together." She gave a half-hearted laugh, "I always imagined we'd get married one day. When he died it broke my heart."

"I'm so sorry."

"I can still see his face; hear his voice. Memories fade but they don't die."

"If it's not too painful, may I ask what the cause of death was in one so young?"

"Pneumonia. It started with the flu and then all went wrong. Poor George."

"Please don't think me indelicate, but many years ago someone wrote *I love Georgie* on the wall inside Holly Cottage. Was that you?"

Mabel smiled. "Did they really? But no, it wasn't me. The culprit was most likely one of the young lads in the village and the Georgie in question would have been Georgina Rowe. She was a good few years younger than me and a real beauty. All the boys were crazy about her."

Meanwhile, Dilly and Amelia went for a walk around the village. On the village green they stopped to look at the War Memorial. "So sad," whispered Amelia. "So many lives lost."

"Yes, and still the world is a troubled place."

"It is. It's been a funny old summer, hasn't it?" Amelia took Dilly's arm as they continued on their walk.

"Yes, yes, it has but there is much to look forward to and I'm especially thrilled to have Denzil and his team starting on my bathroom and kitchen extension next week."

"I can imagine you are. And what will follow. Will you finally agree to marry Orville?"

"Sometimes, Amelia Trewella, I think you're a mind reader."

Amelia stopped walking. "Does that mean yes?"

Dilly's eyes shone. "Yes, that means yes. When the extension is built the house will be far too big for just me. Not only that but I enormously enjoy Orville's company. He makes me laugh and having had Freddie live with me briefly last year made me realise just how precious companionship is."

"And have you told Orville of your decision?"

"Of course, and once we're married he'll put his house up for sale and some of the proceeds will go towards good causes close to his heart."

Just after lunch on Thursday afternoon, a car pulled up outside Holly Cottage and from it stepped Jamie's parents in order to collect the boys and see the house they had heard so much about.

With pride, Jamie showed them Archie Penrose's trumpet which he was determined to learn how to play. Mike proudly held up Archie's cricket bat. He was already a good batsman and hoped the age and history of his new possession would bring him luck. Mike also showed them Mabel's necklace from the days when she was Maggie. A reminder he said of the unusual happenings in Cornwall.

It had been agreed that the remainder of Mavis and Archie's items should stay at Holly Cottage where they belonged. The table lamp, which Larry had rewired, had a new home on the table in the hallway and the cuckoo clock, although it would never work again, hung on the wall to one side of the newly installed French doors. Having dried out, Mavis's prayer book stood on the top shelf of a bookcase and the small picture of the beach at Trenwalloe Sands, painted by Archie and complete with a fresh sheet of glass, had pride of place over the mantelpiece.

While Larry showed his son and daughter-in-law around the garden, Kate phoned the hair salon to book a wet cut. After placing her mobile on the kitchen table she reached for the calendar to jot down the time on the appropriate date. But as she raised her arm to hang it back on its nail, her mouth dropped. No longer did the shadow of Mavis's crucifix stain the paintwork.

"It's gone. It really has gone."

Jamie who had just entered the kitchen to collect his trainers from beneath the table, grinned. "And that's because the case of old Harold has been solved, Granny. I told you it was a sign." Wistfully he looked at the blank area beneath the nail, "Shame we got it wrong though. About Sam Cowling, I mean. I was convinced old Sam had duffed up old Harold because he tried to nick his girlfriend."

Feeling melancholy, having watched the previous day from her bedroom window as the police had dug around the apple tree in her next door neighbours' garden, Joy Williams suddenly felt compelled to pay a visit to the churchyard with flowers for her late husband and her parents. Hence shortly after picking flowers she left her home in Glebe Road with a huge bunch of hydrangeas in her arms. After reaching the churchyard she made her way along the familiar route to the area where her husband's ashes lay; there she discarded the wilted sunflowers left two weeks before and placed the fresh flowers in clean water. As she wiped over the memorial stone with a cloth she spoke to her late husband. "Well, my love, it's all been happening here these last few days and much of it very close to home. I think you'd have enjoyed the drama. The jungle drums have been going flat out and the Harold Jenkins mystery that baffled our parents' generation for many years has been solved at last."

She made her way back along the path to where, tucked beside a wooden bench, stood the headstone denoting the grave of her parents. There with thoughts of Harold tumbling around in her head, she placed the remainder of the flowers in the stoneware vase and then walked back home. Once indoors, with a mug of tea in her hands she made her way upstairs to her bedroom, opened the window and looked out to the apple tree where the only sound was that of birdsong. As she finished her tea she placed the empty mug on top of her dressing table, sat down on the floor and opened the bottom drawer. From it she pulled her late mother's diary for 1943 and turned the pages towards the latter part of the book where she read:

September 10th. Friday.

Went to a dance at the village hall. Wore my favourite blue frock. We were all there and it was great fun but as usual Sam had to leave early to be up at the crack of dawn to do the baking. Pity the dance wasn't tomorrow. He could have stayed then because there's no baking on Sunday so he wouldn't need to be up early. He didn't mind me staying on after he left though because I was with Grace. Her parents said she could have the evening off because they thought the pub would be quiet with the dance on. I danced several times with her lovely big brother, Harold. He's home on Army leave and as big a flirt as ever. At the end of the evening he walked me home after we'd dropped off Grace at the pub en route. He's such a dear.

September 11th. Saturday.

Grace called round this morning on her way back from the bakers. Apparently she saw Sam and someone has told him that Harold walked me home last night. As soon as I heard I knew there was trouble ahead. I was right too because when Sam closed the shop he went looking for Harold and left him with a nasty black eye and told him in no uncertain terms to leave me alone. Silly Sam. Harold's a harmless womaniser and not a threat to him and me. The few times I walked out with Harold meant very little. He's a laugh but Sam and I are for keeps.

September 12th. Sunday.

Sam and I went to church twice today and after Evensong he came back to our house for tea. After listening to the radio he went off home to prepare for another weeks baking.

September 13th Monday.

I've heard on the grapevine that Harold is missing. Apparently Arthur went to call for him this morning but he wasn't home and his bed had not been slept in. His stuff is missing too. It's a mystery but I'm sure he'll come back soon. I must pop round and see Grace.

September 14th Tuesday.

Still no news of Harold's whereabouts but his bike was found at the railway station in St Austell today and now rumour has it that he has deserted. I don't believe it. Poor Grace. She's really upset.

September 15th Wednesday.

Oh dear, still no news of Harold. Nevertheless, today has to be one of the happiest of my life. After I came home from work, Sam and I went for a walk along Lady Fern Lane but half way down the road it began to rain so when we reached Holly Cottage we nipped round the back, took the key from its hiding place and went inside to shelter.

The house felt really strange, eerie like, and I noticed Mavis's crucifix was missing. I knew she hadn't taken it with her because Dad and I helped her pack her things before we took her and the twins to the station in a car Dad borrowed from the farm so they could catch the train to Newbury. I wonder where it's gone. Surely it's not been stolen.

On one of the living room walls, someone had scribbled, I love Georgie. So when Sam spotted a pencil on the mantelpiece he drew a large heart and inside it wrote SC loves AN. He then got down on one knee and asked me to marry him. So romantic. Of course I said yes and when I got home and told Mum, Dad and Auntie Beryl, they were delighted. They all like Sam immensely and to celebrate, Dad opened a bottle of marrow rum. One of five made by his dear friend Archie, who gave them to Dad the day before he went away to war.

THE END

Printed in Great Britain
by Amazon